JUNIOR'S FARM
A TALE OF SARDIS COUNTY
By
T. M. Bilderback

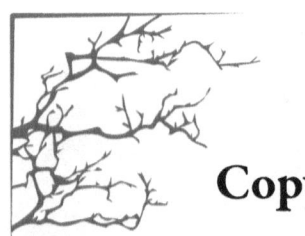

Copyright 2014, by T. M. Bilderback

Connect With The Author
Other Stories By T. M. Bilderback

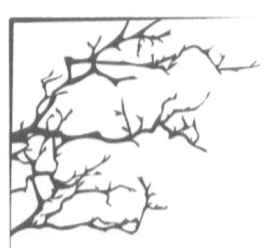

Chapter 1

Katie Montgomery glanced at the gradually receding city in her rear-view mirror. *Sure won't miss that,* she thought to herself. *Nothing there but greed, apathy, and fakery. Time to go be a real person again.*

Having thought that, Katie glanced at her daughter. Carol Grace was sitting in the passenger seat of the late model sedan, ear buds in her ears, listening to music with all the feigned indifference a thirteen-year-old girl could muster. The scene in the kitchen of their apartment when Katie broke the news that they were moving back to Perry had not been a pretty one, and Carol Grace had thrown a fit.

"I am NOT moving to 'Podunk'!" she had shouted. "I don't have *any* friends there, and I simply will NOT be a friggin' farmer!"

"And *you* don't understand, young lady," replied Katie firmly. "Since I got laid off, we can't *afford* to live in this city any longer! Thanks to Gram, I *own* that little farm, with no payments to make and no rent to pay, and we *will* move there while I still have money to move with!"

"*OHHHHHH!*" said Carol Grace disgustedly, retreating to her room in tears.

Since then, Carol Grace had been moping around the house, packing when she had to, and sighing a lot. There hadn't been a lot said between the two for the last two weeks.

Katie sighed. *Oh, Mark, I wish you hadn't died. I could use a little support right now.*

Katie's husband, and Carol Grace's father, had died five years earlier. Brain aneurism. He was probably dead before he hit the floor, the doctors had told her. As if that made it any better.

Mark had life insurance through his company, but it was only a hundred thousand dollars. After his cremation expenses, it had left a good nest egg. She and Carol Grace had been able to continue living comfortably, if not as lavishly.

Two months ago, her employer, Kempco, had decided that they could downsize in the poor economy, and her job had been eliminated. She was able to draw unemployment, but, with no jobs to be had in the corporate-minded city, Katie had begun to dip into the nest egg left by Mark's insurance. She saw that without her steady income, the nest egg would not last.

Her Gram, Nebbie Ballantine, had left her the farm that Gram and Grampy had worked for so many years. Katie had been raised by Gram and Grampy – Katie's parents had been killed in a car accident when she was ten. Grampy, or Arthur Ballantine, was known to most of the community surrounding Perry as "Junior", and had died during Katie's senior year in high school, and, upon Gram's death five years later, just before Mark's passing, Katie had sold off the cows, chickens, and hogs, sealed the house, and gone back to the city. The farm was known to all of the Perry residents as "Junior's Farm", and Katie had only visited occasionally, for summer vacations or weekend getaways.

Gram had passed away suddenly. Katie had received a phone call from Perry General Hospital, and she had actually been able to talk to Gram for a moment.

"I'm on my way, Gram...*please* hold on until I get there!" Katie had begged her grandmother.

"I can't promise, Katie, but I'll try," Gram had replied. The words were obviously taking great effort. "I have something to tell you before..."

Katie never found out what Gram had to say. The heart attack had been a strong one, and Gram's heart just couldn't take the strain.

Those vacations and getaways had become nonexistent after Mark's passing.

The farm was six hundred acres, with a house and seven outbuildings, including a bunkhouse for a hired hand. It was divided into three hundred acres of cropland, and two hundred seventy five acres of pasture and hay-growing fields. The remaining twenty five acres contained the farmhouse, bunkhouse, garden area, chicken coop, hog pen, equipment "garage", tool shed and a big barn. Katie hadn't been there since Mark died.

Now, she was glad she had still kept the farm, and paid the property taxes religiously. There had been offers to buy the place, mostly from big farming outfits, but she had declined them all. The farm was going to be her salvation. Hers...and Carol Grace's.

Katie tapped her daughter's leg to get her attention. Carol Grace, startled, jumped a bit, then pulled the ear buds from her ears and looked at her mom.

"What would you think of getting a dog?" Katie asked.

Excitement showed in Carol Grace's eyes. "Really? A real dog? Could it be mine?"

Katie smiled. "Well, ours...but, I was thinking of maybe an elephant dressed in a dog's costume," she said, mock-seriously. "You could carry it in your purse...of *course* a real dog!"

Carol Grace smiled at the joke. "What kind?"

Katie thought for a minute. "You know, it doesn't really matter. Any kind you want, as long as it can be housebroken and trained. We're going to be on a farm, so size won't matter. And we'll have plenty of time to spend with it, so it won't be lonely. It could guard the chickens, too."

"And the cows."

Smiling, Katie continued. "And the pigs."

"And the sheep."

"And the horses."

"And the penguins."

"And don't forget the kangaroos!"

Carol Grace laughed. "Wow...wouldn't it be interesting to have kangaroos?"

"We are *not* getting a kangaroo."

"How about a seal?"

"I bet he'd be all ready to go."

Carol Grace continued, "And the dog could guard the honey badgers."

Katie, who still laughed at the outrageously narrated Internet video, replied, "Honey badger doesn't care."

"How about getting a horse?"

"Hmmm...it might not be a bad idea to have a couple of horses, just to ride around the place. Although, we could really use the exercise from walking...," Katie said thoughtfully.

Carol Grace squealed, wide-eyed, "*Really?* A horse, *too?*"

"Why not? It's a *big* farm."

"Mom, you're the best!"

Katie smiled at her excited daughter. "Thank you, Carol Grace." She glanced sidelong at Carol Grace. "The, uh...farm doesn't seem so bad now, does it?"

Carol Grace smiled crookedly. "I guess not, Mom. I just hope I can make some friends there."

"I'm sure you will, sweetie."

Katie had either sold or donated most of the furniture from the apartment in the city, because Gram's furniture was still waiting, just as she'd left it, except it was all covered with sheets and dust covers. Their remaining possessions were packed into a U-Haul trailer being pulled behind their car, and in the car itself.

"Mom?"

"Yes, sweetie?"

"What kind of animals will we have on the farm? Seriously?"

Katie laughed. *My daughter, the animal lover.* "Well, for sure we'll have chickens for eggs. We'll try to have a cow or two for milk, and I bet we can find a recipe for good cheese on the Internet. We'll have a dog, and a cat, and a couple of horses. And that's just for us! We'll also have cattle on the farm to graze and fatten, so that we can take them to market...but it will take a few years before they're ready. We'll also raise some hogs, also for market."

Katie glanced at Carol Grace. "How's that?"

Carol Grace nodded, as if coming to a conclusion. "Okay, I can live with that. I'll just think of 'market' as going to another farm or something."

Katie squeezed her daughter's hand. "I used to do the same thing, punkin." Katie laughed. "Gram used to understand my feelings about that, too, and sympathized. Grampy, on the other hand, made fun of me, and made me realize that the reason we raise them is for food, and sometimes they have to be harvested, just like a crop of corn, or soybeans."

She glanced at Carol Grace. "The secret is, don't develop a personal attachment to the cattle out in the field. Or the hogs in the hog pen. That way, you'll be able to separate your feelings about them from where they're going. Does that make sense?"

Carol Grace looked at her mother. "It makes sense, but it still bothers me."

Katie smiled. "It still bothers me, too. But we're going to do it!" she said determinedly.

Carol Grace smiled and nodded.

"What kind of animals would you want, besides what we talked about?" asked Katie.

Carol Grace looked at her mother. "Are you being serious?"

Katie nodded.

"Birds. I'd like all kinds of birds, Mom...turkeys, pheasants, peacocks, ducks...if it's a bird, I'd love to try to raise it, and try to make a few pets out of them."

"We'll see what we can do, Carol Grace. But no bringing them into the house! Turkeys do *not* housebreak!"

SIX HOURS LATER, AFTER three bathroom stops and one quick pass at a fast food drive-thru for a burger, they passed a sign that said, "Welcome To Sardis County! Where YOU Make The Magic!" Just below that, the sign read, "A Nice Place To Live!" *I hope so,* thought Katie.

To Carol Grace, she said, "Ten more miles to Perry, sweetie!"

Carol Grace tried to muster some enthusiasm with her reply of, "Great!" But, she was tired from the trip, and it sounded much more subdued than she meant.

Both mother and daughter were quiet for the next ten miles, until they came to the sign that said, "Perry City Limits".

"Here we are," Katie said simply.

The highway had sporadic small businesses lining both sides, and they were mostly places that catered to low-income people. "WE CASH YOUR CHECK – NO FEE FOR FIRST TIMERS!", "LOANS FOR CAR TITLES", and "BUY HERE – PAY HERE! NO CREDIT CHECK!" signs littered the scenery. Then came the furniture rental companies, several tobacco and lottery shops, and a couple of lonely laundromats. Looming on their left was a big box retailer known for low prices, with several peripheral businesses in a separate strip, and a gas station at one end of the big box parking lot.

"That's new, isn't it, Mom? I don't remember that being here before," said Carol Grace.

Katie shook her head. "I certainly don't remember it," she replied.

Mixed in with the businesses that they had passed along the way were several empty commercial buildings, with a few sporadic weeds growing in their parking lots, and faded "For Rent" and "For Sale" signs in their windows or hanging on their doors.

"This looks bad," said Carol Grace. "It makes Perry look a little...well, trashy."

Katie couldn't disagree. "It does look pretty deserted, doesn't it?" She looked down at her gas guage. "We've got to stop for gas and groceries. There's a market and a small gas station just on the other side of the court square. We'll stop at those places."

As they got into downtown, the businesses all became more localized. They passed the high school, and Katie pointed it out.

"That's where you'll be going, Miss Freshman Of The Year," said Katie.

"Mo-om!" replied Carol Grace.

Katie laughed.

They drove past the Sardis County Courthouse, then the Perry Police Department. Just past the police station, Katie turned left. A block further, and Katie turned into the parking lot of Mackie's Save More Market. The gas pumps were on the side, and Katie pulled to them. She opened her purse and took out her Visa card.

"Want to pump the gas for me?" Katie asked.

"Sure, Mom," Carol Grace replied. "How much?"

Katie smiled. "Fill 'er up, Carol Grace!" She opened her car door. "When you're done, lock the doors and come on in. I need help figuring out our grocery list."

"Okay, Mom. Can I get some Little Debbie cakes?"

"Oh, Carol Grace! Those things have no nutritional value at all!" She paused for effect. "We'll get *two* boxes."

Both were laughing as they got out of the car.

THE FIRST THING KATIE noticed as she went inside Mackie's was the cashier on duty. She was fairly certain that the cashier was Phoebe Smalls. Phoebe had graduated from Perry High School the same year as Katie, and had finished her high school career as head cheerleader. Katie had been popular, but had not even considered being a cheerleader. She felt that her path led to college bound courses, and cheerleading was *not* the way to achieve an education...at least, not an *academic* education.

Rumor had it that Phoebe had become pregnant at a party graduation night. Rumor also said that Phoebe was passed out from alcohol consumption at the time, and didn't know who the father might be.

What followed for Phoebe, according to the rumor mill, was a series of failed relationships, three more children from two different fathers (one of which died from an overdose inside a meth lab), and a lengthy stay in a state-funded rehabilitation center. Phoebe had held on to her four children with the help of her mother, and was trying to make it.

Katie harbored no ill will toward Phoebe, even though Phoebe had acted in high school as if she were the master of all girls. *She probably doesn't even remember me.*

Katie was walking down the first aisle in the market, looking at the peanut butter and jelly selections, when Carol Grace found her.

"Here's your card and receipt, Mom," said Carol Grace.

"Thanks, sweetheart."

"Can we please get natural peanut butter? The kind with no preservatives?"

"I don't see why not."

"What kind of jelly?"

"Your choice, dear. We'll hopefully be making our own soon."

Carol Grace looked at her mother. "Really?"

Katie shrugged. "When I grew up there, lots of blackberries grew all over the farm. I'm sure they're still there. We can plant blueberries and strawberries, and I think there are a couple of peach trees."

"Yum!"

Mother and daughter continued their shopping, stocking up on everything. Katie explained that once the farm was operational, trips to town would be kept to a minimum because of all the work involved.

As they turned into the bread aisle, Katie accidentally bumped her cart into a man that was coming out of the aisle.

"Oh, I'm so sorry," said Katie. She registered that the man had on a uniform, and had a sheriff's badge pinned to his uniform shirt. She looked at his face, and realized that she knew him.

"Aren't you Katie Ballantine?" asked the man.

"And you're Billy Napier!" said Katie happily.

Katie and Billy had been good friends during high school. Billy had been on the Perry High School football team, and Katie had tutored him so that he could pass his classes. They had drifted apart in their senior year, but Katie still considered Billy a friend.

Napier smiled sheepishly. "I am, Katie. It's good to see you!"

Katie, grinning foolishly, said, "And it's good to see you, too! So, do you work for the sheriff?"

Napier laughed. "Katie, I *am* the sheriff."

"Wow! You've done so well! I'm proud of you, Billy!"

Adopting a "hick" imitation, Napier kicked his boot at the floor and said, "Shucks, twernt nuthin', ma'am."

Katie laughed. "Billy, I'd like you to meet my daughter. Billy Napier, Carol Grace Montgomery."

Napier actually took his hat off. "It's a pleasure to meet you, Miss. If it weren't for your mom, I would probably be digging ditches somewhere, instead of what I do now."

Carol Grace giggled. "Hi."

Napier put his hat back on, then gestured to the loaded shopping cart. "Here for a vacation, Katie?"

Katie shook her head. "No, Carol Grace and I are going to make a go of the farm."

"Really?" Napier smiled. "So, Katie Ballantine comes home."

"It's Katie Montgomery now," she replied wistfully. "Carol Grace's father...my husband, Mark...passed away five years ago."

"I'm sorry."

Katie shook her head. "Don't be. I miss him, and so does Carol Grace. But, life goes on. When I got laid off in the city, I decided that bringing Junior's farm back to life was our path to fame and fortune. Or, at least a decent living."

"Gonna be a lot of work," said Napier. "Let me know if I can help with anything, would you? I owe you."

Katie nodded. "You don't owe me a thing, Billy, but I will for sure let you know if I can use your help."

Napier nodded, then looked at Carol Grace. "That goes for you, too, ma'am."

Carol Grace giggled again. "Thank you, Sheriff."

Napier pointed his finger at Carol Grace. "You are old enough now to call me by my given name, young lady. My name is William. 'Billy' for short. And that isn't a privilege granted to very many people your age."

"Thank you, Billy," said Carol Grace.

Katie was smiling at her daughter and her old friend. "Thank you, Billy. I'll probably call you within a couple of days, and offer you dinner...if we can get the house in order."

"And I will surely be there, Katie. See you!"

Napier turned the corner and went about his business.

After he was out of earshot, Carol Grace eased close to her mother. "He's pretty good-looking, isn't he, Mom?"

Katie shook her head. "He was good-looking in high school, too, sweetie...but Billy and I both know that we'll always be just friends."

Carol Grace shook her head theatrically. "That's just too bad..."

Katie stopped, and grabbed Carol Grace's arm. "Wait!"

Carol Grace, concerned, said, "What? What is it, Mom?"

Katie shook her head as if to clear it. "I'm...I'm seeing...a vision!"

Still concerned, Carol Grace said excitedly, "What, Mom?"

Eyes closed, Katie said, "I see...my daughter. She's washing dishes...all alone...for a week!" Katie opened one eye and peeked at her daughter, a smile playing around the edges of her mouth.

"Oh, Mom, stop!" Carol Grace giggled again, realizing that her mother was joking with her.

"Grungy, nasty dishes," Katie continued. "All covered with grease...and burned food..."

Carol Grace giggled, and Katie's heart brightened.

Maybe this won't be so bad after all.

At the checkout, Katie and Carol Grace unloaded their purchases onto the moving conveyor belt. With each "boop" of the cash register's UPC scanning device, the total climbed until, finally, the cashier gave them the total.

As Katie swiped her debit card, she said to the cashier, "Hello, Phoebe. How are you?"

Phoebe looked at Katie with squinted eyes, trying to remember who Katie was. Realization dawned on her, and Phoebe smiled. "Katie Ballantine! How *are* you?"

Katie smiled at Phoebe. "It's 'Montgomery' now, Phoebe, and I'm fine. How are you?"

"Oh, I'm as well as can be expected, I guess. It's good to see you! Are you coming back home?"

Well, great! Now it'll be all over the county by nightfall! Out loud, Katie said, "Yes, we are. We're going to put Junior's farm back to work."

"Well, isn't that somethin'!" said Phoebe. "Well, good luck with that, and come visit us again!"

Katie smiled, and left with Carol Grace. They wheeled the shopping cart over to the car, and packed it all into the back seat.

Returning the cart to the corral in the parking lot, Katie told Carol Grace, "Time to head home!"

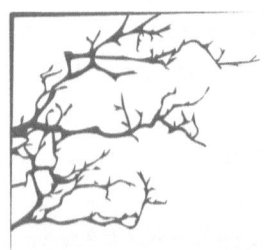

Chapter 2

Katie turned the car into the farm's driveway. The driveway was lined on both sides with a white fence, with apple trees spaced evenly along the length of the drive. The trees had begun growing leaves, since it was late March, and lent a nice effect to the drive. Carol Grace was looking wide-eyed at the scenery.

"Is this all *ours?*" Carol Grace asked incredulously.

"Don't you remember coming here with Dad and I? I think you were eight the last time we came," replied Katie. "But, yes, this is all ours."

They passed a spot that contained a collapsed length of fence. *We'll have to fix that before we get cattle.*

The driveway opened into a large area in front of the house. A giant oak tree stood in the front yard, and a sidewalk led from the front porch steps to the garage and to the parking area. Katie stopped the car in front of the sidewalk. The parking area was made up of gravel, creek rock, and dirt. It could become a little muddy when rain came, but, right now, the parking area was dry.

Katie looked at the house. It was a wood siding house, two stories, with a porch that wrapped around the whole house. The front porch had a swing, and several comfortable rocking chairs were placed around a small, square table. An old English "B", made of wrought iron, was nailed to the wall above the table. Flower beds were on either side of the front steps.

Oh, my gosh! I never noticed before, but it looks just like the house on 'The Waltons'!

"It still takes my breath away," said Katie.

Grampy, I'm sorry, but I'll have to change that 'B' to an 'M' now...or, wait a minute! Maybe I can get 'Junior's Farm' made up of wrought iron or something.

Carol Grace came and stood by Katie's side. "Mom, it's so pretty!"

Katie smiled and nodded while she put an arm around her daughter's shoulders and hugged her. "It sure is, sweetie. Come on, let's go make sure the electricity's on."

They walked up the front steps. Katie started digging through the keys on her key chain, looking for the front door key. She found it, and unlocked the front door.

The house had five rooms on the ground floor. It had a huge living room, kitchen, dining room, den, and another room that could be used as either an office, library, or an extra bedroom. The ground floor bathroom was in the hallway, just off the living room. It was completely furnished, and dust covers protected each piece of furniture. Upstairs, there were four roomy bedrooms, with two more bathrooms. It was a big house for the two of them, but it was worth it...at least Katie thought so.

Katie tried the overhead light in the kitchen. It came on, burning brightly.

"Well, we have power," she commented. "Let's check the refrigerator."

Carol Grace opened the refrigerator. "Looks clean, Mom."

Katie took a look. "It does, but it wouldn't hurt to wipe it out with some very light bleach water."

"I'll do it," said Carol Grace.

"Thank you, sweetie. I'll check the big freezers while you do that. Bleach and rags are under the sink."

As Carol Grace walked to the sink, Katie opened the back door. It led to the porch. The porch along the back of the house was screened in, and contained two gigantic chest-type freezers. Katie opened both – clean, cold, and ready for food.

She went back inside the house to find Carol Grace wiping the inside of the refrigerator.

"I'll start bringing in the groceries," said Katie.

Carol Grace peeked out from behind the refrigerator door. "I'll be done by the time you get back."

"Okay, sweetie."

Katie went outside. She went to the car and grabbed as many of the plastic bags that she could carry. As she walked to the front door, an overwhelming feeling of being where she belonged came over her. The feeling was so strong that she almost started crying.

In the kitchen, Carol Grace said, "Hey, I got it all wiped down, and I dried it with some paper towels. Do you want me to...Mom, what's wrong?" She saw the tears in her mother's eyes.

"Nothing, sweetie. I'm just happy to be here. I feel like I've come home."

Carol Grace hugged her mother. "I'm glad for you, Mom. I'll try to make the best of it, and maybe I'll feel that way, too."

The Montgomery women hugged each other closely in the kitchen.

WITH THE GROCERIES put away, Katie announced that the next item on the agenda was to unload the U-Haul trailer. It would need to be returned the next day.

"Oh, Mom, I'm sooo tired," said Carol Grace.

"So am I, honey, but we've got to get it unloaded. We've got a lot to do tomorrow without having to unload this thing, too."

Carol Grace groaned. "Okay, let's do it."

They opened up the trailer and began taking their things inside.

"Mom, we don't have to put it all away right now, do we?"

Katie thought for a moment. "I guess we can put it off, as long as everything is put into the proper rooms."

"Deal!"

"Look for the box with the sheets and pillows and blankets. We'll need them tonight."

"Will do, Mom."

Gradually, the trailer was emptied. Everything was now inside the house, but on the ground floor. Katie locked up the empty trailer again, then looked to the west. The sun was just touching the horizon. Katie climbed to the porch. The front of the house faced south, and the setting sun was on the side of the house away from the kitchen. The kitchen faced the east, so that it could capture the morning sun.

"Carol Grace!" called Katie. "Can you come out here for a minute?"

Katie pulled two of the rocking chairs around to face the setting sun.

"What is it, Mom?" asked Carol Grace as she came out onto the porch.

"Come sit down for a minute."

The teenager sat down in one of the rocking chairs. Katie sat in the other.

Katie nodded her head toward the sunset. "I know we're in a hurry to get things ready for sleep tonight, and to get some kind of dinner put together...but, take a few minutes, and just look."

Carol Grace turned to look at the sunset. A few clouds dotted the horizon, and the setting sun had colored them in hues of red and purple. A jet contrail crawled across the sky, and the jet twinkled occasionally as the sun caught its reflective sides. "Wow," whispered Carol Grace. "It's beautiful!"

"It is, isn't it?"

Mother and daughter held hands and watched the sunset together, until darkness claimed the farm.

They moved inside then, and Katie said, "Let's go upstairs and choose our rooms."

"I want the one that you used to have, Mom. I remember the window seat."

Katie laughed. "It's yours, sweetie. I hope it brings you as much happiness as it brought to me. It was always my sanctuary...it was the place I went to get away from everything. I spent a good bit of my life in there. I think you'll love it."

The room that once belonged to a girl that had lost her parents, and then her Grampy, faced the front of the house, on the west side. Inside the room, Katie and Carol Grace removed all of the dust covers from the furniture. It was much like Katie had left it.

"You can fix it up any way you want," Katie told her daughter. "Just ask me before you throw anything away."

"Sure, Mom."

Together, they put sheets and blankets on the bed. Carol Grace plugged in an alarm clock, and set the time from her cell phone. The bright red numerals shone from the nightstand.

"Okay, sweetie, I'm going to make up the bed in the master bedroom across the hall, and then we'll go down and find something light to eat that will tide us over until morning."

Katie crossed the hall to the master bedroom. It faced the front of the house on the east side, so the morning light came through the windows. It was, of course, Gram's old room...later, hers and Mark's when they vacationed here. She removed all of the dust covers, then made up the bed. She, too, had an alarm clock that she set from her cell phone. Katie placed her alarm clock on her nightstand. She left the bedroom, and knocked on Carol Grace's door.

"Ready to eat, sweetie?"

Carol Grace didn't answer.

Katie eased the door open. Carol Grace was sound asleep. The teen had kicked off her shoes and had fallen asleep sideways on the bed.

Katie smiled, and went into the room to turn off the light. She shut the door behind her, and went downstairs for a snack.

THE NEXT MORNING, KATIE awoke with the sun peeking through the crack between her bedroom curtains, and the smell of coffee creeping into her room. She smiled, knowing that Carol Grace had gotten up first, and had started breakfast.

The master bedroom had its own bathroom, and Katie took a long, hot shower. She let the water beat down on her shoulders and back to release some of the tension that had built up there over the last couple of weeks.

When Katie had finished her morning routine, she came down the stairs dressed in jeans and a red flannel shirt. In the kitchen, Carol Grace had scrambled some eggs with butter and cheddar cheese, and made toast. The store-bought jelly was on the table, with some spreadable butter. Carol Grace had set two places, and was waiting impatiently for her mother.

"Finally!" Carol Grace said, as her mother came into the kitchen.

"Wow! Look at this spread!" Katie had put her hands on her hips to survey the breakfast that her daughter had worked hard to make. "Eat hardy, Carol Grace Montgomery, because I promise you that we'll have it worked off by lunchtime."

"What's on the agenda, Mom?"

Katie took a bite of the scrambled eggs, then rolled her eyes with pleasure. "Mmm...these are great, sweetie!" She spread butter and jelly onto a slice of toast. "Well, first, we have to take that trailer back. Second, a trip to the high school to get you registered. Since we had your records sent to them from the city, it shouldn't take long. Before you say anything, I'll let you wait until tomorrow to start. That's Wednesday, and should be enough for your first week here. After that, we're back here. We'll check out the barn and the other outbuildings and see what needs to be repaired. Hopefully, there won't need to be much...only that patch of fence that we saw yesterday. But, we'll walk the farm's boundaries just to make sure." She took more bites. "Also, I need to show you the basement...and its secret."

That got her daughter's attention. "Secret? What secret?" asked Carol Grace.

Katie chuckled. "All in good time, Carol Grace. You're old enough to know about it now, without blabbing it all over the place. You'll find out this evening."

"Mo-om!"

THEY RETURNED THE TRAILER with no problems.

When they pulled into the parking lot of the Perry High School and parked, Katie turned to Carol Grace and asked, "Nervous?"

Carol Grace shook her head. "No, not really."

Katie smiled. "Good. Let's get this done."

They got out of the car and went into the front entrance. The office was on their right as they entered. They went inside and spoke to the lady that sat behind one of three desks.

"Hi. I'm Katie Montgomery. I'm here to register my daughter as a transfer student."

The lady looked up. It was obvious that she registered everything about Katie and Carol Grace. "I'll be with you in just a moment. Please have a seat."

Katie looked at her daughter and crossed her eyes. Carol Grace smiled. The two of them sat down.

"Mom, do we have what we need to fix that fence?" asked Carol Grace.

"Probably. At least, as far as wood, screws, and screwdrivers, we should. Paint, on the other hand, would probably need to be something that we pick up today."

"I'm actually excited about the farm now."

Katie smiled. "I'm glad, sweetie. It's time to get Junior's Farm back to work."

The lady at the desk said, "Junior's Farm?"

Katie nodded. "That's right. My daughter and I are going to turn it back into a working farm."

"Then, you're Katie Ballantine."

"I was. It's Montgomery now."

"Oh, I see. And what does Mr. Montgomery think of becoming a farmer?"

"Mr. Montgomery passed away five years ago."

"Oh. I'm so sorry. I didn't know."

"Quite all right...I'm sorry, I don't know your name."

The lady smiled. "No reason why you should. My name is Rhonda Latimer. I started here in the Perry High School office the year after you graduated. I have, of course, heard of you...and your grandparents. They were quite respected around Sardis County."

Katie nodded. "That they were, Mrs. Latimer. Are you from Perry?"

Latimer shook her head. "No, I'm from London."

Basically a hole in the road, London was the small town at the south border of the county. It was incorporated, but they shared water and sewer facilities with Perry, if residents chose to sign up for it. The only thing that London had going for it was its proximity to the east/west Interstate that passed just over the border between Sardis County and the county to the south.

Latimer said, "Come on over, and we'll see if we can't get this girl registered."

The Montgomerys moved over to sit in front of Latimer's desk. Mrs. Latimer picked up a folder that had been on her desk, then looked at Carol Grace over the top of her glasses.

"You are Carol Grace Montgomery?" Latimer asked.

Carol Grace nodded. "Yes, ma'am."

Latimer smiled slightly. "Well. Politeness. Not something I see every day here." She glanced into the folder. "I see you're a freshman."

"Yes, ma'am."

Latimer studied the courses in which Carol Grace had been enrolled in the city. "Everything looks good. We offer all of the same classes, and they should be at about the same place you were when you left. I don't see a problem at all."

Katie said, "Oh, that's good! I was so afraid that something wouldn't be offered, or that she'd have to repeat something that she already had taken."

Latimer smiled. "She's in good shape. Let's get you signed up." To Katie she said, "Will she be starting tomorrow?"

Katie nodded.

"And will she be riding the bus?"

"If possible, yes."

"I'll have the bus driver call you tonight. She will let you know what time she'll pick Katie up in the morning."

"That's very kind. Thank you."

Latimer smiled. "Not a problem. Let me get this paperwork filled out. It will take just a few minutes."

Katie smiled, and when Latimer looked away to do her work, Katie again looked at Carol Grace with crossed eyes. Carol Grace giggled, and when she did, Katie immediately uncrossed her eyes and looked away...just before Latimer glanced up to see what Carol Grace found funny.

A man came into the office, and Latimer looked up and smiled.

"Good morning, Mr. Hendrix," said Latimer.

"Right back at you, Ms. Latimer," replied Hendrix. He nodded toward Carol Grace and Katie. "New student?"

"Yes, she is. This is Carol Grace Montgomery. She'll be taking American History with you...fourth period."

Hendrix smiled. "That's great! I'm assuming you are a transfer student?"

"Yes, sir," replied Carol Grace.

"Wow! Manners! Maybe you need to teach a class here...some of these kids have no manners at all!" said Hendrix.

Carol Grace giggled.

"And is this your mom?" asked Hendrix.

"Yes, sir."

Katie stood, and put out her hand. "Hi. I'm Katie Montgomery."

"She *was* Katie Ballantine," interjected Latimer.

"Katie Ballantine! It's a pleasure to meet you!" said Hendrix, as he shook Katie's hand. "I had the pleasure of meeting...well, I guess it was your grandmother...Nebbie, I think her name was?"

Katie smiled. "That's my Gram."

"Wonderful woman! She always donated to my social studies project each year!"

"I've heard about your project, Mr. Hendrix, and I believe in it wholeheartedly. I would donate this year, but Carol Grace and I have to get the farm up and running first. I need some income before I can give any away."

Hendrix smiled. "I understand. It was nice to meet you! And I look forward to having you in class, Carol Grace."

"Thank you, sir."

Hendrix turned his attention to Latimer. "Have you seen Timothy George today?"

Latimer shook her head. "No, I haven't."

"I think he's skipped school again. He's not on the absentee roster, but he also isn't in class."

"I'll inform Mr. Wallace."

"Thank you," Hendrix said to Latimer. To Katie and Carol Grace he said, "Have a great day, ladies."

"Thank you," they said in unison.

"Mr. Wallace is the principal here," Latimer told Katie.

"Good to know," replied Katie.

AFTER CAROL GRACE HAD received a copy of her classes and meeting times, Latimer had given her directions on how to find her rooms. Katie had paid for lunches for Carol Grace through the end of the school year, gotten a receipt, and they had thanked Latimer for her assistance.

On the way to the car, Carol Grace asked her mother, "Why did you cross your eyes at me, Mom? Didn't you like that lady?"

Katie smiled. "I had heard of her on one of our vacations here years ago. I was told that she was from London, and thought that she could do no wrong." She shrugged. "I felt that vibe while we were waiting. She came across to me as one that could probably bully someone that she felt was beneath her, but toady up to someone that she felt was superior. And she seems...oh, I don't know...kind of...predatory." She frowned. "You know how sometimes you feel an instant dislike to someone, but it's nothing you can put your finger on? It was like that."

Carol Grace nodded as they came to the car. "I know. I don't like her much, either. And I won't say a word to anybody, Mom."

Katie smiled at her daughter as they opened the car doors. "You read my mind, sweetie."

The conversation continued after they got into the car. "So, where to now, Mom?"

"Now, we go to the hardware store on the square for some white paint and a board for the fence, then we go home. We might have just enough time to fix the fence before lunch."

"Great. What about after lunch? Do I get to learn the 'secret' then?"

Katie chuckled. "Probably. We need to make sure the cellar is up to speed, anyway. We'll be storing food there by the end of summer."

Carol Grace smiled. "What kind of food, Mom? Cat food?"

Katie caught on to her daughter's joke. "And dog food."

"And horse food."

"And cow food."

And on it went, until they pulled into a parking space for Knight Hardware, on the court square. They got out of the car and went inside, laughing at some of the outrageous animal food they had come up with.

As they went inside, the bell over the door tinkled. An elderly gentleman came out from behind some curtains in the back and walked toward them.

"Can I help you ladies?" asked the elderly man.

Katie smiled in recognition. "Hello, Mr. Knight. How are you?"

Knight squinted at Katie. "I'm sorry, do I know you?"

"I'm Katie Montgomery. I'm Junior Ballantine's granddaughter."

Knight smiled broadly. "Katie! You used to come in here and haunt the toy department downstairs!" He laughed heartily. "I remember that I used to stock Baby Ruth candy bars just for you! How are you?"

Katie laughed at the memory. "I'm fine, and I surely wish you would stock Baby Ruths again! My daughter is addicted to them, too!" She pointed to Carol Grace. "Mr. Knight, this is Carol Grace, my daughter."

Knight held out his hand, and Carol Grace took it. "It's my pleasure, Carol Grace! I've been in business for almost fifty of my seventy-five years on this earth, but nobody ever brightened up a day like your mother! She was sure the apple of your great-grandparents' eyes, too!" He leaned in close to Carol Grace, and stage-whispered, "She used to go downstairs to our Toyland and play with everything there, almost every Saturday."

Carol Grace giggled. "It's nice to meet you, Mr. Knight. If you can keep Baby Ruth candy bars, I promise I'll be in here as much as I can get Mom to bring me!"

Knight pointed to her. "You have a deal!" To Katie, he said, "What can an old man do for you today, Katie?"

Katie explained about her plans for Junior's Farm, and Knight's eyes twinkled with pleasure.

"Well, I sure am glad to hear that the farm is coming back to life! And by Junior's family, to boot!" He leaned close to Katie. "Now, young lady, you have to promise that you'll buy your supplies hardware from me, and not from that dang undercuttin' big store!"

Katie smiled. "Mr. Knight, I have no plans to shop there. I would much rather pay a few cents more for something I need just to keep the money away from that greedy bunch. A company a lot like them laid me off in the city, and I don't have a lot of sympathy for any overblown, corporate entity right now. Besides, it helps people that I've known all my life to keep their businesses afloat."

"That's right, Katie," replied Knight. "And I guarantee you that they won't hold a charge account for you if you need it, either. And I still have layaway here, too, for big stuff. A lawn mower is a big expense for lots of folks, so I do what I can to help. Now, what color paint did you need for that fence?"

"White, please."

"And a one by twelve board, too, if I remember right."

Katie smiled. "Yes, sir."

"Nails or screws?"

"Screws. They hold better."

Knight started toward the paint, then stopped. "You got a good screwdriver, Katie? Or two?"

Katie smiled. "Yes, I do, Mr. Knight."

Knight nodded. "Jus' checkin'." He went back to the paint, and pulled a gallon of paint from the shelf. He got good three-inch screws on the way back, and set them on the counter. "I'll have to meet you out back for the board, Katie. How long do you need it?"

Katie smiled. "Oh, ten to fifteen years, I would guess."

Knight looked at her curiously for a moment, until the joke dawned on him. He started laughing. "I don't believe it! Nobody's gotten me with that since your Gram died!" The old man held his stomach. "Oh, Katie...that brings back such good memories. Thank you."

Katie and Carol Grace had been laughing at the joke, too. Katie said, "Eight feet, please, Mr. Knight."

Knight nodded. "Good. That way, I won't have to cut it."

Knight totaled Katie's purchases, and directed her around to the back. When she and Carol Grace pulled around back, Knight was waiting with the board.

It would not fit into the sedan.

The three tried turning it several different ways, but the board left several feet of overhang, no matter which way it was turned.

"Tell you what, Katie," said Knight. "If you can wait a couple of hours, I'll load it in the back of my pickup, and bring it out to you when I close the shop for lunch."

"Oh, Mr. Knight, that would be wonderful!"

Knight smiled. "Don't mind a bit. Gives me a reason to visit the place."

"We'll be looking for you, then," said Katie.

Katie and Carol Grace got back into the car and drove home. They waved at Knight as they left, and he waved back, beaming a huge smile at them.

"He's sure nice, Mom," said Carol Grace.

"Yes, he is. He's always been that way. Goes the extra mile for his customers, because they're his neighbors, too. Good lesson for you to learn."

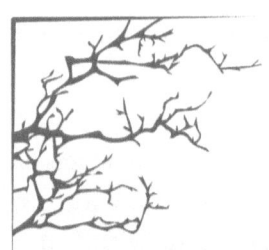

Chapter 3

In the city that Katie and Carol Grace had just abandoned, a man named Alan Blake bet a grand on his poker hand, and it was a honey. He was holding four sevens, and he felt confident that his was the winning hand.

The hand had come down to a duel between Alan and the man across the table.

The man across the table was Moses Turley. He was a high-stakes card dealer and gambler for the Giambini crime family.

Alan Blake was an undercover vice cop, and he was determined to put a huge dent in the illegal gambling going on in the city, under the direct orders of the new mayor, Morris McIllwain.

Alan had determined two big things about Turley.

The man cheated. And the man didn't forgive when someone beat him at poker. A few unfortunate poker winners had turned up floating in the bay, winning hands carefully folded in their shirt pockets and a forty-five bullet in their brains.

Tall, thin, and balding, with long, slender fingers, Turley always wore a "dealer's hat" – basically, an open-topped hat with a green plastic bill. His job was to win as much money as he possibly could, in order to help the Giambini family regain some of its riches, after a recent, stunning gambling loss. The crime family had lost almost every penny it had on a single bet on a World Championship boxing match.

With the FBI monitoring across the street from the main Giambini building, and the renewed pressure from the city's partially corrupt police department, things were getting hot for the Giambinis. They were making desperate choices in their business dealings.

Like killing gambling winners.

Tonight's game was taking place in the office area of an unused warehouse. It was dark and dirty, kept by the Giambinis for various purposes. Six people were playing poker, including Alan's partner, James Winstead. All had folded early in the hand. Besides Turley, there were four Giambini people around the office area, keeping the card game private. Just in case.

Alan could hear a cell phone ringing outside the office area, just as Turley smiled at Alan's thousand-dollar-bet.

Winstead was standing at the makeshift bar behind Turley. He caught Alan's eyes and widened his own, silently asking, "What the hell are you doing?"

"I'll call, and raise you five thousand."

Alan, still confident in his hand, was going to call Turley's bet, when the outside door opened, and one of the guards came inside. He walked over to Turley and bent down to Turley's ear, leaving his back to Alan. The man whispered something into Turley's ear, then pulled away slightly. Turley looked at the man, then nodded.

Alan's nerves began jangling. *Something's up.*

The guard stood, drew a gun from a shoulder holster, and shot Winstead in the chest.

Alan's reflexes were among the best in the force. He drew his service revolver from its ankle holster, and shot the Giambini ape in the head as the goon turned to shoot Alan. Alan stood and put the barrel of his weapon against Turley's forehead before the man could drip his cards.

"Turley, you're under arrest. Now, I'm going to read you your rights: You have the right to tell those other three goons to come inside and drop their weapons, or I will blow your head completely off. You have until I count three. One. Two. Thr..."

A look of hatred was on Turley's face as he called to the three Giambini men. "Tolani! You guys come in! Now!"

From behind Turley came the sound of someone getting to his feet.

Winstead said, "Bastard. Ruined a perfectly good piece of body armor." He drew his gun and waited for the other three to come inside.

Alan reached out and took the cards from Turley's hand, and fanned them out on the table.

Four tens.

Alan's narrowed eyes moved slowly to Turley's. "You cheating son of a bitch," Alan said, matter-of-factly.

Turley shrugged slightly. "Hey, if I didn't, Mickey Giambini would have killed half of the city by now."

Alan used his left hand to take out his cell phone. He called for backup.

KATIE AND CAROL GRACE had just gone to bed on their first night in the farmhouse.

ALAN AND WINSTEAD HAD booked Turley and the three goons for attempted murder. The other four men in the poker game had been held, and were to be placed in protective custody as material witnesses.

After all the paperwork had been filled out properly, their lieutenant had pulled them to the side.

"Great bust, gentlemen," said the lieutenant. "But, I have to warn both of you: Giambini won't take this one lying down. You got orders all the way from the top. The Mayor himself ordered that you two are on vacation until this goes to court, and *nobody* is to know where you are. I mean, *no*-body. You'll call in from time to time and ask only for me or the Captain to get instructions as to when you need to show up in court, and questions from the District Attorney's office will come through us. Use a cheap, prepaid cell phone to call in – the kind you can throw away afterward. If the District Attorney's office insists, maybe we can work out some kind of internet conference with them or something, but it will be from a private place that isn't traceable, and you don't tell them, us, or even each other, where you are, at any time. You will be paid your normal salaries until such time as you can rejoin the force safely. Stay alive, gentlemen...these guys need to go away, and they won't if you don't live to testify."

With little else to say, Alan and Winstead went to the parking lot. They shook hands, and drove away from the police station separately, and in different directions.

Alan did not stop at his apartment. He left in the clothes he wore, figuring he could pick up anything he needed once he got to his destination.

Alan Blake was driving to Sardis County. His best friend would find a place to hide him. After all, Alan had been quarterback for the Perry High School Dragons. His wide receiver, and best friend, still lived there, and could keep his mouth shut, while helping Alan stay disappear.

That's what friends are for, he thought, with a slight smile on his face. *Billy's really going to be surprised to see me!*

KATIE LED CAROL GRACE down the cellar stairs. The lights, thankfully, still worked, and burned with one hundred watt intensity. Gram would never allow dim forty or sixty watt light bulbs in the cellar. She wanted to be able to *see.*

At the bottom of the sturdy, wooden steps, the cellar widened into a huge fifty by twenty-five foot room. Each wall was lined with well-built shelves, each fastened carefully to the cement blocks that made up the walls of the underground storage room.

Carol Grace looked around the room, wide-eyed. She had never been to the cellar before, and Katie hadn't had a reason to visit the room since her grandmother had died.

"Wow, Mom! This place is great! It's huge!"

Katie smiled. "Yes, it is. Now, picture all of these shelves packed to the brim with jelly, preserves, and vegetables, all in Mason jars. That's the way Gram kept it, and that's the way I hope you and I can keep it, too."

"That would be a lot of stuff."

"This farm can grow it, and we can store it. It stays naturally cool year round, so that the food lasts longer."

Looking around, Carol Grace said, "Mom, wouldn't it be better to keep the two freezers down here?"

"It might be something to think about sometime, but right now, we can't move them by ourselves. Those steps don't seem like much until you're trying to maneuver a hundred and fifty pound chest freezer down them."

"Oh. I guess you're right." Carol Grace looked around again. "So, is this the big 'secret', Mom?"

Katie smiled. "Not by a long shot." She walked over to a set of shelves on the far wall. "Come here, sweetie."

Carol Grace walked over to her mother.

"Okay," said Katie. "This is to be our secret. Only us are in the know. Promise."

"I promise, Mom!"

Katie ran her hand under the third shelf from the bottom. "Give me your hand."

Carol Grace reached under the shelf, and Katie took her daughter's index finger. She guided Carol Grace's finger to a large bolt apparently helping attach the shelf to the wall. But, there were *two* bolts, side by side.

"Feel those?" Katie asked.

Carol Grace nodded.

"Push the second one."

Carol Grace, with an inquisitive look on her face, pressed against the second bolt. The shelf made a noise as if a latch had detached, then it hummed. Carol Grace jumped back, startled, as the entire wall slid four feet to the side.

A tunnel, traveling farther than the lights of the cellar could penetrate, was there.

"When I was a little girl, Grampy used to pop up to see what I was up to from time to time. That by itself is not unusual. But, occasionally, Grampy would show up in places like the barn or the chicken coop when I knew for a fact that he was nowhere to be seen outside." She waved her hand toward the tunnel. "*This* is how he did it."

Carol Grace peered inside, looking all around. Two simple on/off switches were inside the tunnel on the left wall. The left switch was labeled "lights" and the right switch was labeled "door". Two feet past the opening of the tunnel, the walls abruptly turned from cinderblock to dirt. "How far does it go, Mom?"

Katie laughed. "All over the farm. There are hidden entrances in all the major outbuildings, and there are also branches going all through the fields. The field entrances are disguised with realistic-looking rocks and brush. The ones in the outbuildings have straw, fake feed bags, or tackle over them to hide them. As near as Grampy could figure out, the tunnels were originally dug back during Prohibition. This property used to belong to rumrunners. Grampy updated and reinforced them so that he could go from place to place when it was raining. That way, he wouldn't get wet, or get mud on his boots. It's also a great place to go during bad storms."

Carol Grace was awed. "Wow." Then an excited look came to her face. "Can we go exploring?"

Katie laughed. "Not today, sweetie. We have to wait for Mr. Knight. He'll be here soon, and we have to fix the fence. When you get home from school tomorrow, we'll explore...and I'll show you each entrance, and how it works."

"Oh, I can't wait!"

MR. KNIGHT, TRUE TO his word, arrived at ten minutes past one. Katie and Carol Grace were waiting for him at the section of fence that needed to be repaired. Mother and daughter had retrieved two Phillips screwdrivers, a battery-powered drill, two four-inch paint brushes, a flat head screwdriver for prying open the paint, and, just in case, a hammer.

Examining the broken rail of the fence, Knight made an observation. "Here's your problem, right here. Looks like something backed into the fence and broke the rail in two. Wood's still good, but I'd say it's been about a year or so since it happened, based on the weathering of the broken edges."

"Who would do that?" asked Carol Grace.

"That's about the time that big farming conglomerate tried to buy the farm from me," replied Katie. "Remember, Carol Grace?"

Carol Grace giggled. To Mr. Knight she said, "I remember him. He was really rude, and very pushy. Mom told the man he could leave our apartment as he came in, or he could leave it as a tenor. He left rather quickly when Mom got her wooden croquet mallet from the closet."

Knight nodded. "Probably scoping the place out, see if it would be worth buying. Can't prove anything, though. Well, then. Carol Grace, you take one end of this new board, and I'll take the other. We'll let your mom put the screws to it while we hold it. Go a lot quicker if I help."

Katie removed the old broken board, and, after a bit of board maneuvering by Knight and Carol Grace, Katie drilled new screw holes, and the board was quickly attached to the fence posts.

"You're on your own with the painting, Katie," said Knight. "I still gotta eat some kinda lunch, and get back to the store."

"Are you sure I can't offer you anything, Mr. Knight? I feel bad that you've come all the way out here."

Knight waved her off and shook his head as he walked back to his truck. "Stop it, Katie. You just help me out when the time comes, and we'll be even. How's that?"

"You have a deal, Mr. Knight. Thank you."

"Bye, girls. See you later, because those Baby Ruths will be in the store by Saturday."

Knight got into his truck and left.

Katie pried the lid off of the paint can, and picked up a good-sized stick to stir it with. As she was stirring, she told Carol Grace, "If we only paint the one board, it will stick out like a sore thumb. We probably need to paint both boards."

Carol Grace shrugged. "Okay."

Katie judged that the paint was mixed enough. She and Carol Grace painted the whole section of fence, on both sides. Then they stood back to admire their work.

"Hmmm. It makes the rest of the fence look faded," said Katie.

"Mom, there is no way we can get that entire fence painted today!"

Katie smiled. "I know, sweetie. We'll just have to live with it."

They packed up their supplies and walked back to the house.

"Come on, daughter of mine. Time to show you the outbuildings...we have to make sure that they're not falling down or anything."

Katie led the way behind the house. The barn was first. It was a good-sized building, with doors that shut comfortably. Inside, it rose high above their heads, with a huge loft. Two different ladders led to the loft, and it had several bales of hay stored there.

Carol Grace could hear some of the hay rustling. "What's that noise, Mom?"

"Maybe squirrels, maybe rats...can't tell from just the noise."

"Rats?" the girl said anxiously.

Katie laughed. "Yes, rats. Every farm has them, sweetie. The only cure is a couple of barn cats. Sometimes, that isn't enough. Let's go back down."

The barn had six stalls. Katie came to the last one on the right. She pointed to the back corner of the stall.

"See those feed bags?"

Carol Grace nodded.

"That's the opening to the tunnel. There's a handle under the bags that you can lift, and the hatch comes up. If you have a horse or a milk cow in this stall, you have to be careful not to surprise them too much, or they'll kick. You don't want to be kicked by a horse. It can kill you if it kicks you in the right spot."

The rear door of the barn opened to a panoramic view of the pasture. Quite a bit of chaff had grown up, and spots of green were showing throughout the two hundred acre field.

"Wow," said Carol Grace, awe filling her voice. "Mom, it's gorgeous!"

Katie smiled. "It is that, Carol Grace." She looked over the acreage for a moment, then said, "A couple of goats, a few cattle, some horses, and a hay baler will whip this pasture back into shape."

"Goats?" said Carol Grace excitedly. "Really?"

"Sure, sweetie, why not? Goat milk and goat cheese are supposed to be really good, and good for you. Come on, let's check the toolshed. It's attached to the barn."

They walked to the toolshed, and opened it. Some of the tools were getting a bit rusty from sitting in the shed for so long.

"We should be able to salvage most of them. Grampy used to rub gun oil into them to keep the rust off. We'll try that, and see what happens. Then we'll sharpen the ones that are supposed to be sharp. Grampy kept them sharp enough to shave with."

Katie locked the toolshed, and they continued over to the chicken coop. Katie found that the building was still sturdy and sound, with thirty nesting boxes, and lots of room for the chickens to roost. The pen surrounding the coop was intact and in good shape. Nothing should keep them from starting with chickens almost immediately. That improved the mood of both mother and daughter.

"Can we get chickens today, mom? Can we?"

"We still have to have new straw for them, Carol Grace. That stuff in the barn is hay, not straw. It may be old, but it still can be good fodder for horses and cattle. We don't even know where to find chickens. No, I'm sorry, honey...it will have to wait a couple of days. But, this afternoon, we can head over to the Farmers' Co-Op and have several bales of straw delivered, if they have any. We can also buy something to keep the chicks warm while they grow. They probably will know who might have chicks for sale, and other farm animals. We'll also go see the Farm Agent, too. First, we have to check out the pig pen, and make sure that it's in good shape. And the equipment garage. I need to make sure that the tractor and the harvester are still in running condition."

ALAN PASSED THE COUNTY line, and saw the sign that said, "Welcome To Sardis County – Where YOU Make The Magic!"

Ten miles to go. I hope Billy's in the sheriff's office.

SHERIFF BILLY NAPIER was not in the sheriff's office. He was at the Farmers' Co-Op, buying dog food. As he threw the fifty pound back of kibble into the back of his pickup, he saw Katie's sedan turn into the parking lot. Smiling, he walked over to the car and opened the door for her.

"Why, thank you, sir," said Katie, climbing out of the car.

"Hi, Katie. Hi, Carol Grace," he said to them. "How does the farm look?"

Katie took a deep breath. "Overwhelming right now, thank you."

Napier laughed. "Got a lot to do?"

They all three began walking toward the store.

"Not as much as it could have been, but, yes. I don't know how we're going to get it all done. I need to plow, plant, and fertilize. I need to get supplies for the animals. I need to get the garden plowed and planted. I need to slop out the barn, the chicken coop, and the pig pen. I need to oil Grampy's tools." She shook her head. "Carol Grace starts school tomorrow, and I don't know if I can do it all."

Holding the door open for her, Napier said, "Maybe you should start smaller. Give yourself a year or two to get everything under control."

They were at the counter. "Nice idea, but I need income *this* year. My nest egg won't last with all of this outlay," said Katie. "Wait a minute. Why are you here? Are you following me around, Billy Napier?"

Napier laughed. "Nope. I raise dogs on the side. I'm here for dog food."

"Dogs?" asked Carol Grace. "What kind of dogs, sir?"

Katie laughed. "I promised Carol Grace that she could have a dog."

"Really? Well. A girl's first dog should be something special. I raise Boston terriers," Napier said. "I think I have just the one for you, Carol Grace. She has papers and everything. All you provide is the love and the housebreaking."

Carol Grace's face lit up. Her excitement was obvious. "I *love* Boston terriers! Oh, Mom, can we get her? Can we?"

Katie shook her head, smiling. "How much will one cost, Billy?"

Napier started rubbing his chin, thinking. "Well, let's see...food...shots...I think...yes, I think twenty-five cents will cover it. One shiny quarter, please."

"Mom? I have a quarter, Mom! May I have the dog?" The teenager was almost jumping up and down with her excitement.

"Billy, you can't be serious," said Katie.

Billy nodded. "I am serious. It's payback for high school."

"But you don't owe me a thing for high school!"

Napier put his hat on his head. "Listen, Katie: I owe *everything* to you! College, the police officer job I had for several years, sheriff...all because one girl took the time to make sure that one poor dumb wide receiver made his grades. I owe you a debt that I'll never get paid off. I consider you a friend, and that's all there is to that."

Flustered, Katie said, "Will you please let me pay you for the dog?"

"Nope," replied Napier. "But, if it bothers you that much, you can owe me a favor. I promise you that someday I'll take you up on it."

Katie shook her head, knowing that between the two of them, she had lost her argument. "All right, I owe you a favor. A *big* favor."

Napier smiled at his friend. "Thank you, Katie. Now, why don't you get done what you need to get done here, and you two can follow me home. Carol Grace can pick out the dog she wants."

To Carol Grace, Katie said, "The dog is *your* responsibility. Feeding, water, housebreaking, the whole nine yards. All you."

Smiling widely, Carol Grace said, "Oh, I'll take care of her, Mom. No problem."

Katie handed her list to the clerk behind the counter, and asked for her purchase to be delivered to Junior's Farm. The clerk assured Katie that everything would arrive that afternoon.

Katie then turned to Napier. "Okay, let's go."

ALAN BLAKE ARRIVED at the Sardis County Jail. He parked his car, and walked inside. To the lady on duty behind the glass, he said, "Hi. I'm looking for Sheriff Napier. Is he around?"

"He's gone to lunch right now, but I expect him back within an hour. Would you like to sit down and wait."

"Yes, I would. Thank you."

Alan sat down in the hard plastic chair and tried to get comfortable as he waited for his friend.

"OH, MOM, THIS IS THE one," said Carol Grace, in between licks on the face from an excited puppy.

"Looks like a good choice to me," said Napier.

Katie shook her head in resignation. "Okay, Carol Grace. She's yours." Katie opened her purse and got out her wallet. She found a new, shiny quarter and gave it to Napier. "Your payment, sir. Thank you. And I owe you one."

Napier smiled. "Thank *you*, Katie."

"We have to go. The man from the Co-Op said that he'd be there soon. I guess I'll take my flea-bitten mongrel with me...and the dog, too," said Katie.

Carol Grace giggled. "Mo-om!"

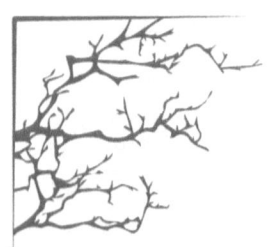

Chapter 4

Alan Blake sat in a slightly more comfortable chair in Sheriff Billy Napier's office. The office door was shut, and Napier had asked that he not be interrupted. Al had explained why he was there, and what he needed.

"So, you need a hole to hide in that you can pull in around you," said Napier. "Someplace nobody expects to find you. That's a tough order, Alan."

"Not really. Only three people on the police force in the city know that I'm from Sardis County. One is my partner, and the other two are my lieutenant and my captain. I don't think any of them are on the Giambini payroll."

"Even so, we need to make sure that *no*-body finds out that you're here. Of course, you can stay with me for a couple of days, but just in case, I'll think seriously about a better place for you to hide out. If they find out about Sardis County, they'll find out about me. My place would be the first to be looked at." Napier leaned back in his chair. "Damn. I know that the Giambinis aren't going to find out, but I hate that there's a chance they could come here!"

"I can go out into the woods, if the situation is too much for you. Maybe old Margo Sardis could hide me," said Alan.

Napier slapped his hand down on the desk. "Jeez, Alan, don't go stirring up *that* old witch! I'd rather face the Giambinis than have *her* throwing her magic around!"

Both men laughed at Napier's remark, but it wasn't far off the mark. Margo Sardis was the last known descendant of the family that the county had been named after. Most of the county's residents thought old Margo was a witch. Not an ugly old woman, but a real, magic-spewing, card-carrying witch. Very few people wanted anything to do with her, and those that sought her out seemed to pay a steep price for her kind of help.

"Want to hang around here until quitting time, or do you want to go ahead to my place?" asked Napier.

"I better head to your place, just to keep out of sight. Listen, do you mind picking up a few things for me? I left the city with just this." He waved his arms up and down, indicating the clothes he had on.

"Sure, give me a list. And some money. I'm not paying for your scabby old self."

THE DELIVERY FROM THE Co-Op was brought to Junior's Farm as promised. The delivery truck backed up to the door of the barn, and the two men would only carry the purchases into the barn. Putting everything away would be Katie's responsibility.

Katie tried to talk the men into putting the straw up in the loft, and the fifty-pound bags of animal feed into the storage area in the barn, but they still wouldn't do it. They explained that the Co-Op only delivered to farms, and that they had too much to deliver to take the time at each farm to put away supplies.

"You need a farm hand," said one of the men.

"Thanks," said Katie, frustrated. She could lift fifty pounds, but it wasn't easy. And at least one bale of straw needed to go to the chicken coop, and the heat lamps that would keep the chicks warm needed to be installed. How in the world was she going to do all of that by herself?

Under her breath, she whispered, "Oh, Mark, I really need you now. Have I gotten in too deep? How am I going to do all of this alone?"

Of course, there was no answer that Katie could hear.

LATER, AFTER DINNER, Katie's phone rang. It was Carol Grace's bus driver, Mary McKinnon.

"Thank you for calling, Ms. McKinnon. What time should Carol Grace be ready?"

"I usually pass by Junior's Farm about six-thirty, Mrs. Montgomery. If Carol Grace could be out by six twenty-five, we should be okay."

"Will you come up the drive, or does she need to be waiting out by the road?"

"Please, out beside the road. It's quicker than trying to turn the bus around to get out of a driveway."

"Will do. She'll be out first thing in the morning. Thank you, Ms. McKinnon."

"You're most welcome. I look forward to meeting Carol Grace."

The call ended, and Katie went to the living room. Carol Grace was in the floor, playing with the puppy.

"Sweetie, I just talked to your bus driver. Her name is Mary McKinnon, and she'll pick you up out at the road. She wants you there by six twenty-five. I think you should be in bed by nine, don't you?"

"Probably so, Mom." Her face lit up. "Can Little Bit sleep with me tonight?"

"Little Bit? Is that what you're naming your dog?"

Carol Grace nodded enthusiastically.

"Fine with me, as long as she knows where to find the puppy pad."

"YOU KNOW WHERE THE bathroom is, right? I don't want you peeing in the potted plant again," said Napier.

Alan replied, "That was you that peed in the potted plant. I peed in your yard boot. And we were ten."

Napier laughed. "I miss those days, Alan."

"Me, too."

"I'm sorry I don't have more to offer than this sleeper sofa."

"Hey, it's a bed, isn't it? Sort of, I mean."

"Good night, Alan."

"Night, Billy. Sleep well. And thank you again."

"No problem, old buddy."

CAROL GRACE'S ALARM went off at five AM. With a loud groan, she reached over, turned on her bedside lamp, and shut off the alarm.

Why is it bothering me today? Yesterday I was up before five, and it didn't bother me a bit! Oh, I know – school. Yuck.

The teen pulled herself out of bed. She looked longingly at Little Bit, who was still buried under the covers, and padded down the upstairs hall to the bathroom. She turned on the shower to let it warm up while she used the toilet.

Let's see...blue or green today? First impression with these kids...I don't want to seem stuck up or anything. Blue. Nice, warm color. Calming. God knows I need to be calm today.

KATIE BEAT HER DAUGHTER to the kitchen, but only barely. Little Bit followed Carol Grace to the kitchen.

"I'm not really hungry, Mom."

Katie smiled. "First day jitters?"

Carol Grace nodded. "*Big* time."

"Okay, then how about some fruit? Think that will get you through until lunch?"

"Probably."

Katie opened the refrigerator freezer compartment, and pulled out a bag of frozen fruit. She popped the bowl into the microwave, and defrosted the fruit. She sprinkled a spoonful of sugar on top, and put the bowl in front of her daughter.

"Better hurry, sweetie. Bus will be here in fifteen minutes."

"Okay, Mom," replied the girl, between bites. "Will you watch Little Bit, please? Help her with her housebreaking? She did really well last night – she peed on her puppy pad, and nowhere else."

"Sure, I'll keep her with me as much as possible. I'm going to try to hook up the heat lamps in the chicken house today, then see if Grampy's tractor will still run."

"Sounds like fun. Want me to stay home and help you?" Carol Grace asked hopefully.

Katie laughed. "Truthfully, I'd love it. But I don't think the school system would be very enthusiastic about you missing school on your scheduled first day."

Carol Grace slumped, faking dejection. "O-kayyy. A girl has to try." She ate the last bite of her fruit, gulped down her juice, and grabbed her books. "Ready!"

Katie hugged her daughter closely. "Good luck today, sweetie. Make it the best first day ever. And, remember: I love you."

Carol Grace smiled. "I love you, too, Mom. Bye!" She trotted her way out the back door and down the driveway to the road.

Katie watched until the bus had picked Carol Grace up safely, then went upstairs to get dressed. She had a lot to do today.

"Come on, Little Bit! Let's get cracking!"

"GET UP AND GET CRACKING, you lazy bum!" said Napier jokingly, as he kicked one of the legs of the sleeper sofa.

Alan groaned. "Noooo. I want to sleeeeep!"

"Uh-uh, you gotta *earn* your keep, old buddy."

"Go away, Billy!"

Napier laughed. "If you don't get out of that bed, you won't have to worry about the *Giambinis* murdering you..."

"No!"

Napier went to the kitchen. When he returned, he had a pitcher of ice water. He held it over Alan's head.

"Last chance, Alan..."

When Alan didn't respond, Napier, grinning broadly, started pouring the cold water over his friend. Alan jumped out of bed swearing at Napier.

When Alan was finished with his swearing, Napier asked him, "Are you through?"

Alan laughed. "Yeah, for now."

"Good. I wanted you out of bed for two reasons, Alan. I have to go to work, and I don't want to leave you here alone and not conscious. I'm really concerned about your safety. Second, if you don't mind earning your keep, some of the dog kennels need to be swamped out, and the dogs let out into the dog run. Would you do that for me today?"

Alan started pulling on jeans and a T-shirt. "Sure, I'd be glad to. How often do you sell a dog?"

"I sold one yesterday."

"Really? How much did you clear, if you don't mind me being nosy..."

"Twenty-five cents. I sold a female puppy for twenty-five cents."

"You're kidding."

"No, I'm not. Do you remember Katie Ballantine?"

Alan looked at his friend. "Katie? The girl that got you through high school? Of course I do."

"She's moved back here from the city, and she has a young daughter that wanted a dog. I let her pick one that cheap because I get the idea that Katie doesn't have a lot of money stowed away. I owe her."

"That's great, Billy! I always thought Katie would have been a good catch. She was cute as a button."

"She's absolutely gorgeous now."

"What's she doing back here?"

"Katie's trying to bring Junior's Farm back to life."

"Wow. I hope her husband knows something about farming."

"Her husband passed away a few years ago. It's just her and her daughter." Napier, who had been walking back toward the kitchen, stopped for a moment. "I've got an idea!"

KATIE KICKED THE TRACTOR tire in frustration.

She had been trying for two hours to get Grampy's old tractor to fire up. She had replaced the battery, checked all of the plug wires, filled the gas tank, and changed the oil, but the machine just wouldn't start.

On the way to the equipment shed, Katie had stopped at the barn with the intention of carrying a bale of straw to the chicken coop. She could pick it up, but it took every muscle she had. Halfway to the chicken coop, she had to put the bale down, and she couldn't lift it again no matter how hard she tried. She had wound up dragging the bale to the coop, grateful that no one was around to see her doing it.

After that, Katie had made two more trips between the chicken coop and the barn, carrying the heat lamp equipment. She began to set it up, but it required a grounded plug, and the receptacle in the chicken house was ancient, and wouldn't accept the three-prong plug. Katie didn't have an adapter.

So, she decided to fire up the tractor, and hitch it to Grampy's old trailer. That way, if she could muscle supplies to the trailer, the tractor could carry them where they needed to be. Since the tractor wouldn't start, that idea was no good.

The morning had been a total bust.

Right after she kicked the tire, Katie heard a car honk its horn. Apparently, she had a visitor.

Katie kicked the tractor tire once more for good measure, and started toward the front of the house. As she got closer, she saw a sheriff's car in the driveway.

Billy.

Sure enough, when she reached the front of the house, the driver of the car turned out to be the sheriff. Someone was with him, and looked vaguely familiar to Katie, but she couldn't place him. He was good looking, too.

"Hi, Katie!" called Napier.

Katie smiled. "Hi yourself, Billy Napier! What brings you out here?"

Napier indicated Alan. "Katie, do you remember Alan Blake?"

Katie's eyes widened in surprise and recognition. "Alan Blake? The *quarterback?*"

Alan chuckled. "Hello, Katie. It's been a few years." He held out his hand to shake.

Katie ignored the hand, and hugged Alan instead.

Alan, surprised, hugged back after a moment. "Wow, Katie, it's good to see you, too."

Katie pulled away. "I'm sorry. It's been a bad morning."

Napier, smiling, said, "Maybe I can help with that. Can we go inside and talk, Katie?"

Katie, puzzled, said, "Sure. I'll make some coffee."

"That would be great!"

IN THE KITCHEN, KATIE had put on a pot of coffee, and invited the two men to sit at the table. The three people made small talk until the coffee was done, and Katie poured three cups.

"I'm making lunch soon, and I expect both of you to stay," said Katie.

"Thank you," replied Napier. He took a sip of coffee.

"Both of you look like you've eaten lemons. Why don't you tell me what's up?"

Alan looked at Napier and widened his eyes. Napier looked at his coffee cup, then began to speak.

"Katie, are you having trouble with the farm? I mean, could you use some help?"

Katie, puzzled, said, "Well, I wouldn't turn it down, if you're offering."

"Have you thought about a farm hand?"

Katie looked at Napier. "I wouldn't be able to afford one, Billy." She looked at Alan. "Are you needing a job, Alan?"

"No. I mean, not exactly," replied Alan.

"Alan, we have to tell her what's going on," said Billy.

"That would be nice," said Katie. "I don't understand what you two are talking about."

Alan took a deep breath. "What I'm about to tell you has to stay in this room, Katie. It's life or death, and it's no joke."

Katie nodded hesitantly. "Okay, you have my word."

"You just moved back from the city, right?"

Katie nodded.

"Have you heard of the Giambini crime family? Mickey Giambini?"

"Yes. They're often all over the news."

Alan nodded. "I'm an undercover cop. The new mayor, Morris McIllwain, gave orders that we are to work hard to keep crime down. I was working undercover to investigate some of their gambling practices, and my partner and I had penetrated far enough to get into a high-stakes poker game with Moses Turley. Someone in the force must have leaked who my partner and I were, because one of his goons tried to kill us at that game. I shot him, and arrested Turley and three others."

"Good! You need to keep criminals off the street!"

"Yes, it's good. But, the problem is the Giambinis." Alan leaned forward. "If this had been just a run-of-the-mill arrest of some nobody, I would still be in the city. But, my lieutenant and my captain are both afraid that the Giambinis will try to kill me, kill my partner, Winstead, and kill the other four witnesses, before Turley goes to trial."

Katie nodded. "No witnesses, no way to prove the crime happened."

"Well, not a sure way. Lots of circumstantial evidence is involved in this case, but, without us, the D. A. would have a really tough time." Alan sipped coffee. "When the lieutenant told Winstead and I to skip out until the trial, and to tell no one where we were, I headed here. I figured Billy could hide me out."

"So," said Katie slowly. "Where do I figure into this?"

Napier moved his coffee cup around nervously. "That part is my idea. Alan needs to lay low until the trial. I figured that you needed help getting the farm up to speed. If you remember, Alan's folks had a farm here."

Katie nodded.

"I thought that Alan could help you out here," continued Napier. "He could hide out, and help out, at the same time. Nobody would ever expect to find him on Junior's Farm."

Katie leaned back in her chair, and looked at the two men. "You want me to hide Alan here, and put not just myself, but my daughter, in danger? Are you two serious?"

Napier said, "Katie, I can't keep him at my place. Even if somebody finds out that he's originally from Sardis County..."

"And that chance is very slim," interjected Alan.

"...they won't know that he's on Junior's Farm," finished Napier.

"The danger would be so small for all of us...," said Alan

"Or we wouldn't have come to you to begin with," finished Napier. "And you can call it *the* favor!"

Katie glared at Napier. "Tell me why you don't want him at your place."

Napier smiled. "If, somehow, they find out about his link to Sardis County, my place would be the first place they'd check. My concern is keeping Alan alive. No one will suspect you, and I have every confidence that he would be safe here. And so would you and Carol Grace."

Katie sighed. "Let me make us some lunch, and I'll think about it." She cut a quick glance at Alan. "Is lunch meat okay? Sandwiches? I have provolone cheese."

Alan, meeting Katie's glance, replied, "I love provolone."

Katie smiled at the corners of her mouth as she rose to make lunch.

LEO LESKO RODE THE elevator to the top floor. He was not looking forward to speaking with Mickey Giambini.

In Lesko's mind, Mickey had lost it. When he lost all that money to the boys in Vegas over that damned boxing match, and when Joey Justice and Justice Security had come here – *here*! Waltzed right in, took Jackie Blue from under their noses, shot Vincent Lambosa in Mickey's office, then put the FBI across the street in the Himes Building...well, it just wasn't pretty to watch the head of the organization melt down.

The last couple of months had been hard on the Giambinis. Everything had to be spoken in code, because the Feds could probably hear what they were saying anywhere in the building. Money had become tight, because of the new mayor's crackdown on crime, and now Moses Turley and his crew had been arrested...thunderheads were gathering around the Giambinis, and the storm could break at any time.

Lesko hoped that he could just stay alive when the storm broke.

The elevator doors opened, and Lesko stepped out. Rizzo, second only to Mickey Giambini, was sitting across the desk from the receptionist. Both recognized Lesko, and Rizzo said, "You can go right in, Leo. He's waiting for you."

"Thanks."

Lesko opened the door to Mickey Giambini's private office. Giambini was doing the same thing that he'd been doing quite often lately...staring out his office window at the building across the street. The FBI had become an obsession for Giambini, and he had added money to the bounty on Joey Justice's head. The price on Justice's head had been originally placed by Esteban Fernandez, the insane Mexican general, and leader of the biggest and most dangerous drug cartel in Mexico.

Giambini feared Fernandez.

Lesko said nothing. He knew that Giambini knew he was there, and that Giambini would speak when he was ready.

"Them sonsabitches," said Giambini, almost to himself.

"Who, Mickey?"

Giambini waved his hand toward the window, and raised his voice. "All of 'em!"

"Gotta agree with you there, boss."

Giambini took his eyes from the window, and focused them on Lesko's.

"What's the latest on Moses?" asked Giambini.

"Bail's been set at two point five million dollars."

Giambini swore bitterly. "Why the *hell* is it so much? And why are you still standing, Leo?" Giambini sat down in his desk chair.

Lesko moved to one of the chairs across the desk from Giambini, and sat down...but *not* in the chair that Vincent had met his fate.

"Boss, my guess is that they're trying hard to turn Moses. Get him to give you up for a little sympathy from the judge."

"You think he's going to turn?"

Lesko shook his head. "No, Mickey. Moses is as loyal as I am."

Giambini threw a thumb toward the window behind him, then winked at Lesko. "I wonder if they're going to realize that this is all trumped up...Moses wouldn't do what they said he did."

Lesko winked back. "Of course he didn't, boss. Here's the report on that load of sausage that shipped out this week." The Giambinis owned a sausage processing plant...it was one of their few legitimate businesses. Lesko leaned forward and handed Giambini a printed sheet of paper.

Giambini said, "Thanks." He started reading it.

The message was simple: *We found all four of the other guys in the game. They didn't hide as well as they should have. Also, we got a lead on one of the two cops.*

Giambini smiled. "This is good news, Leo. I want you to follow through on every aspect of this sale. Put your best men on it, and make it happen as soon as you can. Meanwhile, I'll take care of this report." He flicked his cigar lighter, and set fire to the sheet of paper. "Can't let the competition see these numbers."

The two men watched until the paper had burned down to ash.

Lesko stood. "I'll get right on that, boss."

"Thanks, Leo...things might finally be going our way for a change."

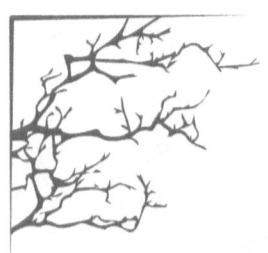

Chapter 5

Lunch was finished.

The three high school graduates had made small talk during the meal. Katie had caught up on several of her old classmates, and found out that everything she had heard about Phoebe had been correct.

After all three laughed at some remark that Alan had made, Napier turned to Katie.

"Made up your mind yet, Katie-skate?" Napier asked, using his old nickname for Katie.

Katie smiled slightly. "Well, it's really against my better judgement..." She looked up at Alan. "But, yes, Alan, you can be my farm hand."

Alan found himself reaching across the table and taking Katie's hand. "Thank you, Katie. I'll do what I can to help you make the farm a success."

She squeezed Alan's hand. "I just want you to *not* get Carol Grace killed. Everything else is secondary."

"I understand." Alan turned to Napier. "Billy, will you help me get my stuff from the car?"

CAROL GRACE'S DAY HAD started off well enough. On the bus, she had to share a seat with a second-grader. That was good – the little girl thought that Carol Grace was *very* cool.

Once in school, Carol Grace enjoyed a little bit of a celebrity status. She was the "new kid", and, of course, everyone wanted to know all about her. Carol Grace was reticent about sharing too much about herself, at least until she saw where the "cliques" were, and how they were divided. She wasn't "cliquey", and wanted friends from all over school...not just the popular people.

Carol Grace also wanted good grades. Especially in high school. Without them, her scholarship chances were slim, and her mom sometimes moved heaven and earth for her, but paying for a college education was way more than her mom could afford by herself.

Carol Grace was more like her mother than she knew.

At the beginning of each class that morning, the teacher asked Carol Grace to stand up while she was introduced. Then, she had to say a little about where she came from, and who her family had been. When she mentioned that she was Junior Ballantine's great-granddaughter, each teacher nodded and smiled. Carol Grace felt each time as if she had been neatly categorized and filed away.

By fourth period – class and lunch – with Mr. Hendrix, she was really tired of talking about herself. Hendrix seemed to sense that, and only introduced Carol Grace. He didn't ask her to talk about any of that mundane stuff, and, for that, she was so grateful.

In the lunchroom, Carol Grace had gotten her lunch tray, and she looked around the cafeteria for a place to sit. Most of the places were taken already, but she spotted a seat at the opposite end of a table in the rear of the room. She began walking toward it, when someone deliberately tripped her. Carol Grace lost her balance, and her tray was jolted out of her hands. Her lunch splattered all over the floor, some splashed up on her clothes, and she barely kept her feet.

Laughter came from all over the cafeteria. Carol Grace whirled around to see who had tripped her. One girl was looking at her with a smirk.

Tightly controlling her voice, Carol Grace asked, "Did you trip me?"

The girl had been in two of her morning classes, but Carol Grace didn't know her name. The girl started laughing.

"I sure did, and you did some fancy dancing!"

"Why?"

"Because you think you're better than everyone else!"

"What in the *world* made you think that?" said Carol Grace loudly. Anger was building in her eyes, and the other girl saw it.

"My mom told me. She went to school with your mom."

Carol Grace got closer to the girl until only a few inches separated them. "I don't even know you!" she shouted. "And you don't know me! Or my mom! But, if it's a fight you want, I'll be more than happy to give you one you'll never forget."

Carol Grace reached down to the girl's plate, lifted it, and casually turned it upside down over the girl's head. Food spilled all into the girl's hair and across her face. Carol Grace then calmly placed the upside down plate on top of the girl's head and stepped back.

Silence filled the cafeteria, with the exception of the plopping noise of food hitting the floor.

The girl took the plate off of her head, wiped spaghetti sauce off of her face, and looked up at Carol Grace. The girl launched herself from her chair, and she tackled Carol Grace. Both girls fell to the floor.

The fight was *on!*

"YOU CAN STAY OUT IN the bunkhouse, Alan," said Katie. "It has everything you'll need – dishes, electricity, a firm bed, bathroom, running water, and, if you don't want to eat with Carol Grace and I, a hotplate. There's a wood stove for heat, and a big window air conditioning unit for this summer."

"Thank you, Katie. I'm sorry about all this."

Sheriff Napier had helped Alan retrieve his belongings from his car. Alan and Katie had said goodbye to the sheriff in the driveway. As Napier drove away, Katie and Alan had begun walking toward the bunkhouse.

"It's okay, Alan," replied Katie. "I plan to work you like you haven't worked in years, though. You'll earn your place. Are you any good at wiring? Or getting tractors running?"

"Yes to both, but not in a long time."

Katie explained about wiring the heat lamps. "I really want to get that going. Carol Grace has her heart set on raising some chicks. I want to get her started as soon as I can. And the tractor won't start." She explained all she had done herself that morning. "If we're going to get the field plowed in time to plant, we're going to have to hurry...but we can't do it without the tractor."

"I'll fix it. Where's your pickup truck?"

Katie hesitated. "I don't have one."

Alan looked at her. "You're kidding."

Katie shook her head. "I know I need one. If I get a little time tomorrow, I may go see if any car dealerships will trade a decent used truck for my sedan. The sedan is last year's model, and it's paid for, so, *maybe...*" She let the sentence dangle.

"Maybe they will. Even if you have to pay a little bit more to get the truck, we really need one here."

"I'll see what I can...," said Katie, but didn't finish the sentence. Her cell phone was ringing. She dug it out of her jeans pocket, pressed the "answer" button, and said, "Hello?"

KATIE WAS SHOWN INTO Mr. Wallace's office. The principal was seated behind his desk. He was a short man, with wavy black hair, wearing a sport coat and tie.

Across the desk from the principal, two girls were seated in chairs that were covered with plastic trash bags. One of the girls was Carol Grace, and both girls were covered with what looked like spaghetti and spaghetti sauce. She looked at her mother sheepishly.

Katie said, "Hi, I'm Katie Montgomery. What's going on?"

"We're waiting for one more parent, Ms. Montgomery," said Wallace. "We'll cover the particulars once she arrives. Please sit down." Wallace indicated a small couch.

Katie, puzzled, sat down.

Within a couple of minutes, the door to the principal's office opened, and Phoebe Smalls was shown in.

"I got here as soon as I could get. I was at work," said Phoebe.

Wallace indicated the same couch that Katie sat on. "Please sit down, Ms. Smalls."

Phoebe noticed Katie already seated, and a surprised look crossed Phoebe's face. Katie interpreted it as an "Oh, crap, I know what this is about" look.

Wallace stood.

A thought crossed Katie's mind. *He's the same height standing or sitting!*

"Ladies, I have called you here to address a situation that occurred today at lunch." Wallace leaned against his desk. "These two girls got into a fight."

Phoebe exclaimed, "Oh, dear!"

Katie said nothing.

"From what I can determine, Mary started the fight by tripping Carol Grace."

Mary Smalls looked at a point on the principal's carpet. Carol Grace kept her attention on Wallace, since her mother was seated behind her.

"Mary then, apparently, made the situation worse by saying that her mother had said that 'some people think they're better than others', or something to that effect."

Phoebe looked everywhere except at Katie. Katie looked at Phoebe, and felt the anger building.

"Now, I can't force you two ladies to work out your differences, whatever they might be. But, as for your daughters, I can. Or, at least, I can make sure that they know how to get along with each other. So, the consequences of this little fight today will be the following..." Wallace paused until he had both girls' attention. "I'm going to have your schedules rearranged. You will attend all classes together, you will go to lunch together, and you will be assigned to sit together at lunch and in your classes. You will spend all of your school hours together until I see fit to change it. You will either learn to get along, or I can expel both of you. It's your choice. Make it now."

Carol Grace didn't hesitate. "I choose to get along."

Mary said angrily, "I'll take that, too."

"Good," said the principal. "You will both go home for the rest of today. In the morning, you begin spending your time together with a one-week in-school suspension. You will be tutored, and you will keep up with your homework. After the week is up, you'll begin your other consequences. Now, if you'll step into the outer office, please. I want to speak to your parents."

Carol Grace and Mary rose, and left the office.

Wallace turned his attention to the two women. He stood up from the edge of the desk, pulled up a third chair, and placed it facing Katie and Phoebe. He sat, and looked from on to the other.

"I understand that you two ladies were classmates, and graduated together from Perry High." Wallace looked at Phoebe. "I looked through the annuals for each of the years you two were here. I saw that you were a cheerleader." He shifted his gaze to Katie. "And I saw that you were a Ballantine, and that you were smart enough to be a member of the Beta Club. So...what I'd like to know, considering that both of you were among the top students of your graduating year, is just who thinks they're better than anyone else?"

Katie was the first to speak. "Certainly not me. I'm not responsible for the 'smart' genes that I inherited, and I come from a long line of farmers. I have been lucky, but I have never...," she turned to Phoebe, "*never*...thought I was better than anyone. I have no reason."

Phoebe turned to Katie. "Oh, really? I saw the way you looked at me in the checkout line! You barely spoke, and you looked at me as if I were nothing!"

"I did not! I didn't speak much because we were never close! I had nothing to share with you!"

"Oh, but you sure 'shared' it with Billy Napier, didn't you? Just like you 'shared' it with him in school!"

"Billy has never been more than a friend to me, Phoebe. All I did for him was help him learn, so that he could keep his grades up and stay on the football team!"

"Oh, sure! I don't believe a word of that!"

Realization dawned on Katie. "You *like* Billy, don't you?"

Phoebe looked around, then down at her hands. "Maybe."

"And you're jealous of our friendship?"

Phoebe sobbed, and began crying quietly. "Yes, I'm jealous. Why doesn't he look at me? *Notice* me?"

Katie opened her purse and took out a tissue. She gave it to Phoebe. Phoebe wiped her eyes and said, "Thank you, Katie."

Katie quietly said, "Phoebe, have you ever just *talked* to Billy? Told him how you feel?"

Phoebe sniffed, and shook her head. "He doesn't see me. He wouldn't look at me that way." She looked into Katie's eyes. "Besides, he probably thinks I'm a drunk. Or a slut. I've almost lost my kids because of partying, and he probably thinks I'm no good."

"Has he ever said that to you?"

Phoebe shook her head. "No."

Katie looked down at her hands, and made a decision. She looked up at Phoebe, studying the woman.

Phoebe Smalls was still a good-looking woman. If her past was really her past, and there was no risk of falling back into drinking, maybe...

"Phoebe, let me help you," said Katie.

"No, I'm not taking any money from you," responded Phoebe. "I don't take charity like that."

"Good," replied Katie. "I don't have any money to give you." She put her hand over Phoebe's. "I was thinking about trying to fix things for you...with Billy."

Phoebe's eyes widened. "Really? How?"

Katie smiled. "Just put yourself in my hands, Phoebe. I'll do what I can. But, first, let's go see our daughters, and let them know that there aren't any problems between us. Okay?"

Phoebe smiled. "Thank you, Katie. I'm sorry for what I said."

"Not a big thing, Phoebe," replied Katie. "But, let's go straighten the girls out before they escalate to the point of no return."

The two women stood. Wallace, forgotten by both women, stood, too.

"If there's anything more that I can do for you ladies, please let me know," said Wallace.

The two women laughed as they left the office.

"BUT, MOM, I DON'T WANT to be her friend!" said Carol Grace on the way home. "She tripped me on purpose, and said that we thought we were better than anyone else!"

"Carol Grace, for the last time, it was all a misunderstanding!" replied Katie. "Phoebe has always been that way...she'll get an idea in her head, and it takes an act of Congress to change her mind."

Carol Grace crossed her arms and slumped into the passenger seat. "Just because you and her mom have made up shouldn't mean that I have to. I don't even *like* Mary Smalls!"

"You don't know whether you like her or not. You just met her today."

Carol Grace sulked as Katie turned the car into the driveway.

"Doesn't matter, Mom. I'm *not* going to like her, and I'm *not* going to be her friend!"

Katie shrugged as the car came to a stop. "Suit yourself. But *you* are the one that's going to have to spend every school hour with her...until you two learn to get along."

"Fine!" Carol Grace left the car, slamming the door, and headed toward the barn.

Katie shook her head. *Might as well let her have her fit. She deserves it after today.* Katie went inside the house, and headed for the kitchen.

Katie froze as Carol Grace screamed, and ran from the barn, coming for the house at a full run. Little Bit came running from the barn, too, barking and chasing Carol Grace happily.

"Mom! Mom! There's a man in the barn! Mom!"

Katie looked worried, until she remembered that she had given Alan a place to lay low.

Alan came from the open door of the barn with a perplexed look on his face, and straw in his hair. He began walking toward the back door of the house too, bringing up the rear.

Katie almost burst out laughing.

Carol Grace slammed the back porch door hard enough to bang the side of the house with a loud *SMACK!* And almost immediately flung the kitchen door open, terror in her eyes. Little Bit was barking merrily.

"Mom!" cried Carol Grace. "There's a man in the barn, and he...Ohh! There he *is!*" The teen hid behind her mother as she pointed to the kitchen door. "Mo-om!"

Alan had seen Katie through the kitchen door window, and came inside.

Carol Grace screamed.

Little Bit began barking even more.

Alan started trying to speak, to ask what was going on.

Katie couldn't help herself...she started to laugh uproariously. It had all struck her as something from an old movie. An old screwball comedy, maybe.

Alan and Carol Grace shared a simultaneous look of amazement, and both said, "What's so funny?" in unison.

Katie found that even more funny, and doubled over with her laughter. She stumbled backward until her legs hit one of the kitchen chairs, then she fell backward into it, surprised. This sent her into even more laughter.

Both Alan and Carol Grace began to smile. Little Bit had sat down in front of Katie, and was looking at Katie with her head tilted severely to the right.

Alan looked at Carol Grace, and said, "You must be Carol Grace."

Carol Grace nodded.

"I'm Alan Blake. I went to school with your mom...and with Billy Napier. We graduated together. Your mom has agreed to let me help out with the farm for a while. I didn't mean to surprise you."

"Mom didn't tell me." Carol Grace looked at the floor. "I'm sorry I threw that hay at you, Mr. Blake. You scared me."

Alan laughed. "You have a great arm! That straw hit me right in the face!"

Katie, who had begun to calm down, heard this, and renewed the gales of laughter.

Little Bit tilted her head sharply to the left, still looking at Katie.

Both Alan and Carol Grace began laughing, too. It was contagious.

"LOOKS LIKE WITNESS number two, Lieutenant," said the police detective.

Lieutenant Stanfield Pyne swore with variety and bitterness. Of the six men that were to testify against Turley, only Alan Blake, James Winstead, and two other men remained. Each of the two witnesses had been systematically murdered, and the killings had been fairly gruesome.

As gruesome as the murders had been, the killer or killers had been careful to make certain that each victim could be identified easily. Pyne thought at first that the killer was taunting the police department, but, after further reflection, he discarded that idea. He finally decided that the reason was two-pronged: one, to let the police department know that they should leave the Giambinis alone, and, two, that no witnesses would be left to testify against Moses Turley, no matter what actions the department took to protect them.

Pyne swore again, told the detective to continue processing the murder and to keep him informed, and left to call his captain.

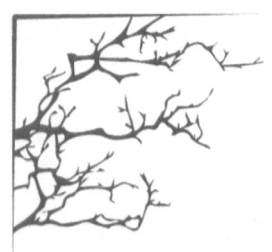

Chapter 6

"And that's why your mom is letting me stay here," said Alan.

Carol Grace looked at the table. She shot a couple of glances at Alan, and then glanced at Katie. Katie nodded, reaffirming what Alan had said.

"And you're a friend of Mr. Napier?" asked Carol Grace.

Alan nodded.

"And he knows you're here?"

Alan nodded again.

Carol Grace flashed a fast glance at her mother. "And he doesn't mind?"

Alan smiled, and Katie blushed.

"Carol Grace!" said Katie, flustered. "What a thing to..."

Alan interrupted. "I got this one, Katie." He smiled again. "Carol Grace...Billy doesn't mind that I'm here. Billy has no interest in your mom romantically. I mean, *zero!* He's never been interested in Katie that way. They're friends, and that's all." Alan paused. "He's my best friend, and has been since...well, since always. And I would know." He thought to himself, *Now, me...I've had a crush on Katie since...well, always. But you won't ask me that. I hope.*

Immediately proving Alan to be a liar, Carol Grace asked, "Okay...but do *you* like Mom that way?"

Now it was Alan's turn to blush. He opened his mouth to say something...*anything*...when he was saved by Katie.

"Carol Grace Montgomery! What a thing to say! Especially after you've just been sent home from school!"

"But, Mo-om!"

"Don't 'but, Mo-om' me, young lady! You go to your room right now, and I don't want to see you until dinner!"

"Mom!"

"*Now,* young lady!"

Growling an inarticulate "OHHHHHH", Carol Grace stood up and stamped her feet angrily on each step as she climbed the stairs to her room. Little Bit barked once, then followed Carol Grace upstairs.

When she heard Carol Grace's bedroom door slam, Katie turned to Alan. "I'm sorry, Alan."

Alan held his hands out. "What's to be sorry for?"

"Carol Grace. She's got a fast mind, and her thoughts usually come out of her mouth before she thinks things through."

"She's still a kid, Katie. It's to be expected. May I ask what happened in school?"

Katie put her hand over her brow, mostly covering her eyes. "Oh, wow...Okay, I'll tell you, but you can't say a word to Billy. Deal?"

Alan laughingly said, "Hey, it's a deal on my part! Are we pulling something on Billy? I really *need* to pull some kind of prank on Billy!"

"Do you remember Phoebe Smalls?"

"Feeble Smalls? You bet I do! Billy used to get mad when we called her that!"

Katie looked at Alan in disbelief. "Feeble? You guys had a nickname for her?"

Alan chuckled. "Of course! The whole team would call her that, and you should have seen Billy! He'd get so mad, he'd look like Yosemite Sam from the Looney Tunes cartoons! He had this *huge* crush on Feeble!" *A lot like the one I had...have...on you.*

Katie said, "Oh, I'm *so* glad to hear that! Maybe this won't be as hard as I thought! Here's what happened today..." She told Alan what had happened with Carol Grace, and what she planned to do about Phoebe. "Can I count on you to help?"

"Of course I'll help you! Billy needs this!" said Alan. *And, maybe, just maybe...you'll realize how I feel about you,* he thought. "Wait!" he cried, snapping his fingers. "I almost forgot! The chicken house is ready for egg-laying residents anytime...I fixed the lights while you were gone. Also, the barn and pig pen are both ready for animals."

Katie widened her eyes and stared at Alan. "You're kidding! That's *great!*"

"One thing: before you stock animals, you'll need feed. Or some kind of silage. They can't eat stuff from the grocery store."

Katie laughed at the idea of running down to the supermarket and picking up some microwave pig food. "Alan, that's great news! Let's make some calls, and start populating this place! And, if we can get the tractor running, we can make some hay bales. We shouldn't waste what's in the fields."

Alan nodded. "Agreed."

Katie found the Co-Op's phone number, dialed it, and asked questions about buying chicks and other farm animals. She made notes, and thanked the person on the other end. She disconnected that call, then dialed another number. After a few minutes of discussion, she disconnected the call and turned to Alan.

"Great! Tomorrow we go to check out some chicks! But, don't say anything to Carol Grace, please. I want it to be a surprise!"

"Sounds good to me, Katie! Now, let's go check out the tractor. I might need an extra pair of hands."

"Sure. Let me get Carol Grace, and we'll see if you can use *two* extra pairs of hands."

MICKEY GIAMBINI WAS talking with Rizzo.

"Rizzo," said Giambini. "You know that project we're working on?"

"Sure, boss."

"How's it goin'?" Giambini had asked Rizzo to eliminate the four nobodies. Moses Turley would take care of the two cops.

"It's goin', boss. Slow and steady. Sales are down." Rizzo held up four fingers.

Giambini raised his eyebrows. Rizzo had eliminated the four nobodies. "That's bad, Rizzo," he said, as he gave Rizzo the universal hand signal for "OK". "We gotta find a way to increase sales."

Rizzo grinned. "I got an idea, boss. I think I'll be completing a major sale tonight. Maybe it'll see us through the month. That'll be a lotta meat."

Giambini smiled at his bodyguard. "Hey, the more meat we get rid of, the better. You know what I'm sayin'?"

"OKAY, CROSS YOUR FINGERS," said Alan, sitting in the seat of the tractor.

"And your toes," said Katie.

Carol Grace giggled. "And your eyes!" she said, as she crossed her eyes.

"Hey, kid, your face will freeze like that," Alan told the teen.

"I hope so," replied Carol Grace. "Two of everything is great!"

Alan shook his head. "Okay, here we go!" He turned the key in the tractor's ignition. It began turning over. Suddenly, something in the engine caught, and it fired up, belching black smoke out of the dual exhausts. Alan pumped his fist and said, "Yes!"

Katie and Carol Grace began dancing little boogaloos while saying, "Oh, yes! Oh, yes!" Alan put the tractor into gear and drove it out of the equipment shed. Hopefully, for the last time. He was going to start parking the tractor in the barn, to at least keep it mostly out of the elements. He leaned over the side of the tractor and said as much to Katie.

"Great!" replied Katie. "After you get it stowed away, why don't you come to the house with us? I'm going to start dinner. You're welcome to join us."

Alan nodded, and fed gas to the tractor. It rolled along the dirt path leading to the barn and the house. Little Bit chased after the tractor, barking happily. Alan drove carefully, making sure that the puppy didn't accidentally jump under the tractor's big tires.

When he got to the barn, Alan came to a stop, put on the parking brake, and climbed down. He looked back along the path. Katie and Carol Grace were about halfway to the barn. Alan opened the two big doors, and parked the tractor inside. He turned the engine off, proudly confident that the machine would start quickly the next time he needed it.

"Little Bit!" called Carol Grace. "Come on, puppy! Let's go inside!" To her mother, she said, "What's for dinner, Mom?"

"Spaghetti, salad, and garlic bread."

Carol Grace nodded. "Good. Maybe I'll get the spaghetti into my stomach, and not on someone else's head."

RIZZO FINALLY LOST his tail. Whoever had been following him had been good, but Rizzo was better.

Word had reached Rizzo that one of the cops, James Winstead, was hiding out with his cousin in an apartment a few blocks off of Hooker Hollow.

Rizzo guessed that he'd have to kill both of them. The idea of killing a cop didn't bother him at all. He'd done it before, and he realized that if he was careful, no one would ever tie it to him. The cops would know that it was for Turley, of course...but *knowing* it and *proving* it were two different things.

Rizzo decided to park at McFeely's Bar, known on the city streets as McFeelme's, and walk to the apartment. That way, if anyone was watching Winstead's building, he'd maybe see them first.

As he walked, Rizzo whistled tunelessly and happily. He was fiercely loyal to Mickey Giambini, and he enjoyed his job tremendously.

OVER DINNER, KATIE told Carol Grace about the improvements that Alan had made to the chicken house and the other outbuildings, and the plan to find some chicks the next day.

Carol Grace was excited.

"Chickens? Really?" Carol Grace squealed with excitement, and bounced in her chair, clapping her hands. "What kind, mom? And will we have a rooster? One that crows and everything?"

Katie couldn't help but laugh at her daughter's enthusiasm. "Yes, sweetie, we'll have a rooster...but only one! More than that, and we'll problems with them fighting."

"What will we do with any extra roosters?" asked the teen.

Alan jumped in. "I'll take care of that for you, Carol Grace. Okay?"

"How?" Suspicion was beginning to show on her face.

"We-ell...," began Alan.

"You're talking about eating them, aren't you?" said Carol Grace with accusation in her voice.

"Yes, we are, Carol Grace," interrupted Katie. "We talked about this, sweetie."

"I know, Mom," said Carol Grace, with a frown and downcast eyes. "It won't be easy..." Then she peeked up, and a small smile played at the edges of her mouth. "But he'll be tasty, won't he?"

Katie moved her head in a kind of nod, surprised at this change of heart. "He will be that, sweetie."

"Then I just won't get attached to the roosters," said the teen as she left the kitchen and bounded up the stairs to her room, leaving the two adults to goggle after her, mouths open in disbelief.

Closing her mouth, Katie said, "Was that Carol Grace, or an imposter?"

"I'm not sure, Katie," replied Alan. "Listen, while we're in town tomorrow, I really need to do two things: I need to check in with Lieutenant Pyne, and then I need to go to the sporting goods store...or to the evil big box store. I would prefer a sporting goods store, though. They're more likely to have what I need."

Katie nodded. "I don't see a problem with that, Alan."

RIZZO GOT BACK INTO his car and started it up. *The boss is really gonna be happy,* he thought to himself.

Winstead had been in the apartment, but the cousin was not. Rizzo couldn't believe his luck.

After a little bit of "conversation", Rizzo learned that Winstead didn't know where the other cop, Blake, was hiding.

But, Winstead *did* offer a suggestion as to where Blake *might* be hiding.

Rizzo smiled. Once he learned that information, he had ended poor Winstead's suffering quickly, with a quick bullet to the brain.

Moses Turley's little "problem" could end in as little as a day.

All it would take is a little trip to Sardis County.

The boss might even throw in a little bonus for this one!

KATIE HAD BEEN SOUND asleep that night, when something awakened her.

Someone was in one of the rocking chairs on the front porch. She could hear it creaking back and forth rhythmically.

Eyes wide open, wishing she had thought to think of a fast way to get Alan's attention out in the bunkhouse, Katie eased out of bed. Rather than fumble around with her tennis shoes, she padded barefoot to Carol Grace's room, and slowly opened the door.

Carol Grace was sound asleep, covers askew, and snoring lightly.

Hmmm...I wonder if it could be Alan? But, he wouldn't have come up here without telling me. Would he?

The only way to find out was to slip down the stairs and take a look.

Quietly, slowly, one step at a time...taking each step on the left side to keep them from creaking as they took her weight, Katie made it downstairs. She still heard the steady creaking from the rocking chair. Slowly, deliberately, she tiptoed to the front door.

As she reached for the doorknob, she thought, *Do I really want to do this?*

She looked around, and realized that no one else was lining up, ready to do battle in her place. A giggle threatened to bubble up from her throat, but she quickly quashed it.

Katie turned the knob slowly, making no sound. She realized that she had been holding her breath, and let it out slowly. Gently, she opened the front door. Its well-oiled hinges were silent. Through the screen door, the sound of the rocking chair was louder. As she reached for the screen door, intending to gradually push it open, a voice startled her badly.

"I know you're there," the voice said. "I've come to talk with you, Katie Ballantine. Come sit with me a spell."

Katie, heart beating wildly, pushed the screen door open a couple of inches...just enough to see the rocking chairs.

The moonlight revealed a woman sitting in one of the chairs. The woman was old and hunchbacked. Her hair was sparse, gray, and tied into a bun on the back of her head. It had been years since she lost her last tooth, and her face had a wrinkled, pinched look. Her nose had been broken at one time, and leaned permanently to her right side. An ornately carved wooden cane was firmly planted between the old woman's legs, and her hands rested on it. The cane moved back and forth with the motion of the rocking chair. The glasses on her face could properly be called "spectacles", because they were thick, and, in the bright light of the moon, magnified the woman's eyes tenfold, so that she resembled a grounded owl. She wore an ankle length yellow skirt, sneakers, and a clean, but worn, red pullover sweater.

Katie felt no threat from the woman. She continued out onto the porch, and gently shut the screen door, so it made no noise.

"Do I know you?" asked Katie quietly.

The old woman tilted her head as she looked at Katie. "You should. We met once, you and I. You were only four years old."

Katie studied the woman's face, then shook her head. "I'm sorry, ma'am, but I don't remember you."

The old woman indicated one of the empty rocking chairs. "Then, sit down, child, and I'll give you some history."

After a moment, Katie decided that she wasn't in any danger. She walked casually over to one of the chairs, and sat down.

The old woman smiled. "Oh, child, you look *so* much like your grandmother!" The woman closed her eyes. "But, I can *feel* your grandfather. He's so much a part of you, and you don't even know it, do you?"

Katie shook her head. "No, ma'am, I *do* know it. Junior Ballantine raised me, along with Nebbie, after my parents were killed in a car crash."

"How far back do you remember your family, Katie? On your father's side, I mean."

Katie's brow furrowed, and her mouth turned down into a frown, as she thought. "I remember my great-grandmother, but just barely. I think it was at my great-grandfather's funeral, but I can't be sure."

The old woman nodded. "That sounds about right. Molly passed away about a month after her husband died. Her broken heart just gave up. It was tough on your grandfather, losing both of his parents so close to each other." She shook her head in sad remembrance. "Did Junior ever tell you anything about his mother?"

Katie thought, then shook her head. "Not that I can remember. Neither did Gran."

The old woman shook her head sadly. "They never told your father, either, Katie, and it was the death of him. He didn't know how to deal with what was happening. He had no warning, and no one to talk to about it. That car accident was probably not an accident, Katie. Your father was driving, and he may have driven off that cliff on purpose." The woman looked sideways at Katie, as if expecting Katie to get angry.

Katie, however, surprised the woman. "I've heard that before. The police speculated about it because there were no skid marks, and that the car was travelling more than the speed limit, based on the trajectory. I've come to terms with it, either way."

"Then let me get back to your grandfather's family. Katie, your great-grandmother, Molly, was my sister. That makes me your great-great aunt. Molly Ballantine, before she got married, was Molly Sardis. I'm Margo Sardis. We are descended from the founders of this county, and I'm a witch, as was your great-grandmother, your grandfather, your father, and you." The old woman leaned forward. "And so is your daughter. Carol Grace."

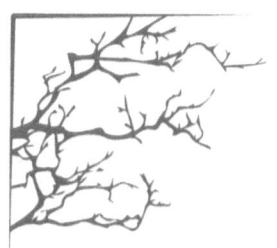

Chapter 7

Katie laughed out loud. "Oh, my God! You have *got* to be kidding me!" She stood and looked down at the old woman. "Ms. Sardis, if that's who you are, you are sadly delusional! Witches do *not* exist! Not outside of a bad movie, or a fairy tale. So, please, leave my property now, and I won't call the police."

"Sit down, Katie."

"I don't think so. I asked you to leave, and if you..."

"*Sit* DOWN!" interrupted Margo. As she said "DOWN", she banged her cane down on the porch, and a blue flash erupted from it, and wrapped itself around Katie. "*Now*, please."

Katie found herself sitting against her will. The blue flash covered her, and she did not have control of her muscles.

"Child, you are my great-great niece, and, though you do not carry the name, you are still one of the last descendants of the Sardis family. You will be respectful to your family elder, do you understand?"

Katie nodded, without the blue glow forcing her to.

"Now, if I release the hold on you, will you sit and listen, or will you still try to fight me?"

"I'll listen."

Margo Sardis glared at Katie for a moment, then nodded. Margo tapped the cane against the porch once more, and the blue power moved back to the cane.

Katie found herself able to move freely again. "How did you do that? Or am I dreaming?"

"This is no dream, child."

Katie looked into the old woman's eyes. "Then, you're really a..."

Margo nodded. "A witch."

Shyly, Katie asked, "Are you a good witch, or a bad witch?"

"I am neither. I am both. I have a nodding acquaintance with God, and with his nemesis, too. I am simply...a witch. No more, and no less."

"But, aren't most witches...well, evil?"

The old woman chuckled to herself. "Katie, witches are how they are based on their personality...just like everyone else." She stopped rocking for a moment. "Some have called me evil...but those that say that are only angry that I gave them exactly what they asked for. I didn't ask 'em why they wanted it, or what their intentions really were. People will ask for things in general instead of exactly what they really want, so I accommodate them. Sometimes, I've had to fix things back to normal...at least, as much back to normal as I could...because of that."

"I used to hear your name back in high school, and that you were a witch," said Katie. "I never believed that you were a witch, and I never had any idea that we were related!"

"Your grandparents chose not to tell you about your heritage, or the power you have inside. I kept quiet, respecting my nephew's choices. When your parents died, I approached him again about telling you. He asked me to please hold off, that they would tell you one day. Then, you went away to the city, and they died. Your visits here became few and far between." Margo shifted in her chair. "I sure wish you had some cushions on this chair, child. But, now you're back for good, and the farm will begin to draw power from you."

"What do you mean?"

"Your grandfather put this farm under a spell. Did you ever notice that the plowing was always done quickly? That his animals never got sick? That he always had a bumper crop of whatever he planted?"

"Sure. I always thought it was odd that he could get the plowing done in a day's time. Usually while I was at school, too."

The old woman cackled. "Junior did that on purpose. He'd act all tired and whatnot that day...and he probably *was* tired. But it wasn't from riding a tractor all day. It was because he had to keep focused on the magic. Sometimes it would get away from him, and he'd have to fix it." She cackled again. "You should have heard your grandmother fussin' at him when it *did* get away from him!"

Katie watched the woman as she laughed. *This* has *to be a dream. There's no such things as witches, and there's no way in the world that I'm one. And neither is*

Carol Grace. So, the conclusion is that I'm dreaming. She surreptitiously pinched her arm. Hard. It hurt. *Okay, so I* dreamed *that it hurt.*

"This is no dream, child," said Margo, as if she had read Katie's mind. "Look up here."

Katie lifted her eyes to meet Margo's.

"You have trouble coming to you, Katie."

Katie looked confused. "Trouble? From where?"

"I cannot tell you. The repercussions would be far too great. But, trust me. Trouble is coming, and it will be up to you and Carol Grace to face it down. I will help you, but I don't know *when* it's coming, so you two may be all there is. I don't want to frighten you, but I will teach you things you can use to protect yourself. Once I've shown you what to do, we will both instruct Carol Grace how to use her power. If we don't, one day when she gets mad, it may explode from her...and we can't have that."

"I still don't quite believe any of this, Aunt Margo," said Katie cautiously.

The old woman smiled. "Ahh, so it's 'Aunt Margo' now. You believe more than you think, child." She leaned over and handed a piece of paper to Katie. "Take this."

Katie took the piece of paper. When she looked at it in the moonlight, there were words written, but not in a language that she recognized. "What is this, Aunt Margo?"

Ignoring the question, Margo asked, "Are you right- or left-handed?"

Curious, Katie said, "Left."

"Hold your hand out like this." Margo held her left arm straight, pointed at a right angle from her body. Her palm was aimed away from her body, and her fingers were curled.

Katie copied the move.

"Now, say the words written there, child," said Margo.

"But I can't pronounce them!"

"Try. The pronunciation will come to you naturally."

Katie shook her head in disbelief, then tried to say the words. To her surprise, they *did* come to her naturally. When she finished saying them, she felt something inside her moving, forming into a solid, pulsating mass. The mass then moved to her arm, and seemed to shoot from her palm in a blue flash, as if the blue power had been shot from a gun. Katie let out a small scream of surprise, then watched the blue light grow until it circled, she assumed, the entire farm.

"Aunt Margo! What...what *was* that?" asked Katie.

Margo smiled at her great-great niece. "What do you *think* it was, child?"

Katie pondered for a moment. "It...it felt like...a protection spell."

Margo actually clapped her hands in happiness. Katie noticed that the cane remained standing even though the old woman's hands were no longer holding it in place.

"Wonderful, Katie! I told you that it would come naturally to you! For all we know, you've been doing that for years, without knowing what you were doing!"

Katie shook her head in bewilderment. "I wondered why we were never burglarized in the city."

Margo nodded. "That's right, Katie! You probably were doing it in your sleep or something." She pointed at the paper. "That particular spell will only last until morning. You will have to repeat it every night. You or Carol Grace."

Katie's eyes widened. "Do you really think that Carol Grace can do this, too?"

"We'll find out at sundown tomorrow, child. If she can't yet, you'll have to do it yourself. It will keep you through the night. Now, you go back inside and get some rest. I'll come back in a day or two, and I'll bring books to show you what to do."

Katie stood, and Margo pushed up gradually from her chair.

"Aunt Margo, would you like me to drive you home? It's very late."

The old woman cackled. "No harm will come to me, child. Am I not a witch?"

Katie smiled. "May I hug you?"

The old woman smiled at Katie. "You'd better hug me, girl. You and Carol Grace are all the family I've got left!"

Katie hugged the old woman. She felt a spark between them as they touched. As they separated, Margo looked into Katie's eyes.

"Be safe, child, and be *aware!* The trouble will come when you least expect it, but if you're prepared, you'll be able to deal with it easily. I'll help you with it, of course. And don't forget to teach Carol Grace what she needs to know about the protection spell."

"Yes, ma'am," replied Katie.

Margo looked deeply into Katie's eyes for what seemed an eternity. Finally, she nodded, as if to herself. "Good night, child. I'll return in a day or two, and teach you more."

Katie nodded as the old woman made her way down the front steps. Katie watched as Margo Sardis walked slowly down the long driveway, until she was only a memory from the moonlight.

Katie went back inside the house, locked the front door, and went back upstairs to bed. She began drifting off to sleep again, confident that the entire encounter with Margo Sardis had been a dream.

THE NEXT MORNING, THE sun shone brightly down on Junior's farm.

Breakfast for the three of them was finished quickly, and Carol Grace was off to catch the bus.

Katie reminded her to be nice to Mary Smalls, and to try to make friends with the girl.

"Mo-om!"

"Don't 'Mo-om' me, Carol Grace. The girl needs a friend, and I can't think of a better one than you." Katie smiled as she said this. It had the desired effect.

"Oh, all right, Mom. I'll do my best."

Alan interjected, "If you don't mind my saying, the two of you together would be an unbeatable team. At least, if there's a spaghetti war, you will."

Carol Grace tried to look angry, but wound up giggling as she ran out the door.

Katie looked shyly at Alan. "Thank you, Alan."

Alan smiled back. "Glad to break the tension. She just needs a reminder to have fun, and that things like what happened yesterday aren't the end of the world." He put the breakfast dishes together, and carried them to the sink. When he had set them down, he turned to Katie and said, "Ready to go get some chickens?"

STANFIELD PYNE FELT goosebumps rising on his skin. He was looking down at the body of Detective James Winstead.

Winstead's body was seated in a leather recliner, with the back tilted back slightly. The detective's eyes had been removed, and placed carefully on one leg. His tongue had also been cut out, and placed on the other leg.

The message was clear: Winstead would be keeping silent about what he saw.

"Lieutenant?" said one of the forensics workers.

Pyne was wondering what the captain would say about this. He was also worried that Winstead may have somehow told the Giambinis where to find Blake.

"Lieutenant?" the forensics guy repeated.

If Winstead had told the Giambinis where Blake may be hiding, then the case against Moses Turley would be over soon. The Giambinis wouldn't stop until they'd found Blake, and eliminated him, too. And the bad part is that Pyne couldn't contact Blake to warn him. He just had to wait until Blake called in.

This was *not* a good thing.

"Lieutenant!" said the forensics guy loudly.

"What? What is it?" said Pyne.

"Sir, we're ready to move the body, unless you want to go over the scene again."

Pyne shook his head. "No, do what you have to do. I'm done here."

The lieutenant briskly turned and left the apartment, saying a quiet prayer that Blake would call soon.

"TWO *hundred* chicks? Are you sure we can handle that many?" asked Alan.

Katie grinned. "Sure! Why not?"

"We'll have to keep an eye on them almost all the time, or we'll lose way too many."

"Carol Grace can help with that. She'll love it."

"Whatever you say, Katie."

"The man even threw in a couple of fifty pound bags of feed...how could I resist?"

"We'll have more eggs than we'll know what to do with. I guess we can sell some."

"Sure...gotta pay you somehow."

"Katie! I'm not on the farm for your money! I won't take a dime, because you're helping me hide from the low-life..." He stopped when he saw the grin on Katie's face. "You imp! You're messing with me!"

Katie tilted her head to the side, smiling broadly. "Whatever makes you think that, Alan?" she asked as innocently as possible. Then she burst out laughing.

Alan shook his head. "I just can't believe how easily you played me."

"Sir, I resent that implication!" said Katie with exaggerated outrage.

They both started laughing.

The farmer that was selling them the chicks chose that moment to walk up to them. With a smile, he said, "Nice to see a married couple still able to laugh with each other."

Katie blushed. "We aren't married, sir."

Alan, whose face was also beet red, agreed. "No, sir, we're not married." *Yet.*

The farmer chuckled. "Sorry, folks. You just look so...right...together. Like you belong with each other."

Katie, embarrassed, said, "Let's get these chicks loaded and take them home."

Later, with boxes of chicks in the trunk, and with more in the back seat, they started driving back to Junior's Farm.

"Alan?"

"Hmmm?" he replied, distracted.

"Can we talk?"

He turned his attention to her. "Sure, Katie."

Katie took a breath. "When we were in school, do you remember any talk about..." She paused for a moment.

"Talk about what?"

"Did you ever hear any talk about...Margo Sardis?"

Puzzlement crossed Alan's face. "You mean the witch?"

Katie nodded.

Alan thought about it. "Well...just the usual stuff. She's a witch, don't mess with her, she'll snatch your children away...that kinda stuff." He glanced at her. "Why?"

Katie frowned. "I dreamed about her last night. Or, at least, I think it was a dream."

"Tell me about it."

Katie told Alan about the dream, all the way up to the old woman fading out of sight in the moonlight.

"Hmmm...So, Katie Montgomery is a Sardis? *And* a witch?" Alan smiled. "Are you messing with me again?"

"No. I'm sure it was a dream, Alan. But, it seemed so *real!*"

"I can see three ways to check it out."

"What?"

"We can check out three things to see if it was a dream, if it's troubling you that badly."

"How?"

"First, we stop at Billy's office, and ask him to check the birth records at the courthouse. They're bound to have your grandfather's birth on record, and a record of his parents."

"Okay. Yeah, good idea. Let's do that, while we're in town."

"Second thing. When we get home, show me the piece of paper."

Katie had forgotten about the piece of paper, or what she had done with it. Then, it suddenly hit her – she had put it on her nightstand when she returned to bed...at least, in her dream, that's where she put it. She explained this to Alan.

"Great, Katie."

"What's the third thing?"

"Repeat the process."

"You mean, try to make the spell happen again?"

"Sure! Everything else can be explained away. But, if you can do it again, then you'll know that it wasn't a dream."

Katie, with a smile playing around the edges of her mouth, glanced at Alan. "You don't seem too upset about any of this."

Alan shrugged. "Hey, I already think you're beautiful, and smart, if you haven't already figured that out. I always did. And, if you're a Sardis, *and* a witch?" He looked at Katie. "What's not to like? All I could hope for is that you like me, and are as interested in me, as I am in you."

Katie blushed as she turned the car into the sheriff's parking lot. *Okay, Katie, here we go!* "Alan, your hopes are right on target."

Katie got out of the car, smiling to herself. Alan followed her, once he got over the realization of what Katie had said.

BILLY NAPIER LOOKED at the two of them with no expression on his face.

"Well, I can answer one question for you, Katie: Margo Sardis is real, she lives deep in the woods, and rumor has it that she's a real witch. Now, as far as you being descended from the Sardis clan, I can find out with a phone call."

"Please do, Billy," said Katie. "I need to know. If Junior's mom was a Sardis, I'd like to go find my aunt, and invite her to the house."

Billy smiled a lopsided smile. "Sounds like she already knows the way." He reached for the phone.

"Hey, Billy, before you call, can I ask a favor?" interrupted Alan.

"Sure."

"Do you have an untraceable cell phone? You know, one of those cheap, prepaid things that can be tossed after a couple of calls? I really need to check in with the lieutenant."

Billy opened one of his desk drawers and reached in. Wordlessly, he handed Alan a clamshell-wrapped cell phone.

"Package is open, but only to charge the phone and add the minutes. With my compliments, old buddy."

Alan smiled. "Thanks, Bill. Please excuse me." Alan left the office.

Again reaching for his phone, Billy said, "Now, let's get you taken care of, Katie."

WALKING AROUND THE parking lot as he dialed the borrowed cell phone, Alan felt a small thread of anxiety growing in his stomach.

Something bad was coming.

Alan sometimes had hunches. Often, these hunches proved correct...and every good cop had them.

The problem with this hunch was that Alan didn't know if it was Katie's "dream" meeting with Margo Sardis, or if it had something to do with the need to check in with his lieutenant. Maybe it came from another direction...one that he didn't know about.

The number Alan had dialed was the direct line to Lieutenant Pyne's office, and Pyne answered on the third ring.

"Pyne."

"Hi, Stan. How's the old card game?"

"Alan?"

"One and only."

"Oh, thank God!"

Alan felt a cold chill along his spine at the tone in Pyne's voice.

"What's happened, Stan?"

Pyne hesitated, then spoke with sadness. "Winstead's dead, Alan."

Alan's felt like someone had punched him in the stomach. "How?"

"The Giambinis got to him somehow. He didn't hide well enough."

"Oh, no, Stan!"

Pyne took a breath. "They've gotten to the other four guys in the game. You're our last witness against Turley, Alan."

Alan overcame his shock and his sadness over the loss of his partner. "I understand, Stan."

"Listen, Alan," said Pyne. "I don't want to know where you are. But, could Winstead have given the Giambinis a hint about your location?"

Alan thought hard. If they had really worked on James, he would have told them. Assume the worst.

"It's possible, Stan. But it would only *be* a hint...a general area. Not an address, because James didn't know one."

Both men were silent. Finally, Pyne said, "Alan, be careful. You've *got* to stay alive until the grand jury convenes. Otherwise, Turley walks."

"When does the grand jury convene?" asked Alan.

Pyne told him.

"Okay. I'll be there, Stan. Count on it."

RIZZO WAS DRIVING MICKEY Giambini to Kenzie's Restaurant. Kenzie's was near the docks in the city. Giambini and Rizzo often went for drives, because Giambini's car was swept for explosives and transmitters several times a day. It was a safe place to talk.

"Sardis fuckin' County? What the hell is that fuckin' cop doin' there?" said Giambini angrily.

Rizzo, remaining calm, said, "I dunno, boss. But that other cop said that's where Blake came from. Makes sense that he'd go hide out there."

Giambini was silent as he stared out the back window, thinking. As the car pulled into the restaurant's parking lot, he spoke.

"Rizzo, go get Turley. Tell him about Sardis County. Tell him that this one's his problem. If he finds the cop, great. If he don't, I wash my hands of him." He reached for the door handle, then stopped. "Start lookin' for another dealer. Tell Lesko to start lookin', too. I don't think we're gonna have Turley much longer. Even if he finds the cop, he's too much of a liability. If Turley *does* find the cop, I want Turley to take care of him. I want *you* to take care of Turley, Rizzo. If he makes it."

"Sure, Boss."

The two men got out of the car and went into the restaurant.

BILLY HUNG UP HIS PHONE.

"Congratulations, Katie. You're a Sardis."

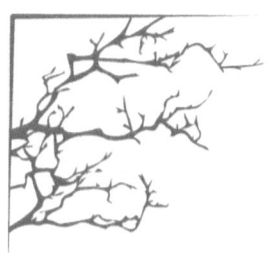

Chapter 8

Carol Grace felt as if she started her day in prison.

True to his word, Mr. Wallace had rearranged schedules for both Carol Grace and Mary. He met both girls at the door that morning, and personally escorted them to the I.S.S. room. The I.S.S. teacher, Mrs. Buckner, was introduced to the girls, and Mr. Wallace left.

"Mr. Wallace has left strict orders," said Buckner. "You two will sit at a table in the back, with only each other for company. You will spend your day studying, doing homework, or reading. You may speak to each other only to discuss schoolwork, and that will be done sparingly, and with my permission. I enjoy quiet. Lunch is at eleven o'clock in the cafeteria. You will sit together, again with only each other for company. You may speak as you wish in the cafeteria, but, when you return here, the talking rules are in effect. Each infraction of these simple rules will add an extra day to your isolation. I suggest that you exercise good judgment. Now, please sit down at the table in the back."

Carefully ignoring each other, Carol Grace Montgomery and Mary Smalls walked to the back of the room and plopped down into their chairs. Both opened their backpacks, both took out their World History books, and began working on their current chapter. As they read, they soon discovered that they were reading at about the same speed, and were actually turning the pages in their books at the same time. Both girls noticed this at about the same time, and each released a dramatic and frustrated sigh. Each girl reached into her backpack, and each noticed the other doing the same thing. Their eyes met. Each girl slowly pulled a book into view.

Both girls had chosen their English Literature book.

Wide-eyed, they stared at each other. Mary held up one finger, meaning "let's try it one more time". Carol Grace nodded. They opened their backpacks, looked in, glanced at each other, and reached in.

Both girls pulled out their Algebra books.

Carol Grace felt wild laughter bubbling up inside her. Mary could see it coming, and shook her head desperately, pointing to a sheet of paper one of them had laid out for homework.

Carol Grace fought hard, and finally stifled the laugh. Her face was red from the effort. She picked up her pen and nodded slightly to Mary.

Mary wrote, "What is going on?"

Shaking her head, Carol Grace wrote, "I have no idea!"

Mary: "Something has to be causing this!"

Carol Grace: "It's like we're puppets or something!"

Mary nodded, then wrote, "I wish Mrs. Buckner would leave for a few minutes so we can talk!"

Carol Grace nodded, and wrote, "Me too! I wish she'd get the runs or something!"

From behind them, the girls heard a chair scrape violently against the floor. They whirled around to see what caused the noise, only to see Mrs. Buckner walking briskly toward the door with her hand obviously trying to hold her butt cheeks together.

"Behave yourselves, girls! I'll...oh...ohhhh...be back shortly!" said Mrs. Buckner.

The teacher left the room.

Carol Grace and Mary looked at each other, wide-eyed and open-mouthed. They both began smiling, then high-fived each other while they laughed.

Mary said, "Carol Grace, I don't know what's happening, but I sure like it!"

"I don't have a clue, either, Mary...but I like it, too!" Carol Grace thought for a minute. "It's like everything we wish for happens!"

Both girls stopped laughing.

Mary said quietly, "Do you think we should wish for Mrs. Buckner to stop having the runs?"

"I wouldn't want her to get sick," replied Carol Grace.

"Me, either. I wish she'd come back now."

"Me, too."

The door opened, and Mrs. Buckner walked back into the room, glanced at the girls, and sat at her desk to read.

The girls exchanged meaningful glances. The friendship had started...and would soon be cemented.

BILLY WAS WALKING KATIE outside. Katie was still trying to wrap her mind around the fact that she was descended from the Sardis line. Did that mean that her dream about the visit from Margo...*wasn't* a dream?

The implications of this revelation flooded her mind. It would have explained a lot of what happened around the farm when she lived there.

But why would Gram and Grampy keep this hidden from her? What had they been afraid of?

And, Katie thought, *if I can do what I did last night...what* else *can I do?*

She and Billy found Alan leaning against the car, staring worriedly at nothing.

Katie noticed that something was bothering Alan. She touched his arm and looked into his face. "Alan, what's happened?"

"Yeah, what's up, buddy? I bet it's not bigger than this, though: Katie is a Sardis!"

Alan looked up, distantly at first, then more sharply as the realization of what his friend had said. He took Katie's hand and held it tightly. "Really? Is it just like...?"

Katie began nodding, and finished the sentence. "...just like Margo Sardis told me. I'm beginning to think that wasn't a dream, Alan. But, I want to know what's happened? What was your phone call about?"

Alan hesitated, took a deep breath, and decided to tell them everything. "I called in to Lieutenant Pyne to find out when the grand jury convenes...and to just generally check in. Pyne had bad news. The Giambinis have killed all of the witnesses against Moses Turley...except for me. They got James Winstead last night. And, the worst part of it is that James may have mentioned Sardis County as one of my possible hiding places. Pyne said that Winstead had been worked over pretty good." He looked down. "I hate to say it, but James would have talked, if the pain was enough."

"Oh, man, that's rough," said Billy. "What do you want to do?"

"Well, they haven't found me yet," said Alan. "I figure if I lay as low as I can, chances are good that they won't find me. But...we can still get prepared. Katie, do you mind if I hang with Billy for a while? Can you get the chicks all taken care of without me?"

Katie nodded, and said, "Of course I can!"

To Billy, Alan said, "Can you drive me around a while?"

"Sure."

"Katie, go home. I'll be there later this afternoon...okay?"

Katie nodded her assent. "I will, Alan. Please be careful." Then, she stood quickly on her toes and quickly kissed Alan's lips.

Both men's mouths were wide open as Katie drove away.

MRS. BUCKNER ESCORTED Carol Grace and Mary to the school cafeteria.

"You have thirty minutes to eat lunch. You may sit together or apart, as you choose. You may talk as you choose. I expect you back in the room in exactly thirty-five minutes. Understood, girls?"

"Yes, ma'am," said both girls in unison.

Buckner turned and walked away in the direction of the teacher's lounge.

Entering the cafeteria, Carol Grace and Mary were chattering away about that morning's happenings. They had tried a couple experiments after Mrs. Buckner had come back to the room, and the result had always been the same.

So, the girls came to a conclusion: something was watching over them. And it was granting their every wish, and was keeping them out of trouble.

At least with Mrs. Buckner. So far.

In the lunch line, Mary said to Carol Grace, "Wow. I sure hope there's an empty table."

"Me, too," replied Carol Grace.

As they left the line with their trays, some other students vacated a table. The girls took it.

Carol Grace said, "Hey. What do you think about coming out to the farm this weekend?"

"I'd like that, Carol Grace."

"Maybe Mom will let you stay all weekend. That is, if your mom doesn't mind."

"Mom won't mind. I think, after yesterday, Mom's changed her tune about your family. And I've changed my mind about you," said Mary.

"Oh, I hope so!" replied Carol Grace. "I know I was sure wrong about you, Mary."

"Awww...isn't that sweet?" said a voice from the aisle beside the table. "The new girl is getting all chummy with the crack whore's daughter! It just...it just warms the *heart!*"

The speaker was a girl, obviously a couple of years older than Carol Grace and Mary. She was dressed in a cheerleader's outfit, and was very pretty. Her auburn hair was pulled back into a ponytail. An embroidered dragon, spewing fire from its mouth, adorned the front of the cheerleader dress, with "PHS Dragons" in a circle around its head from dragon shoulder to dragon shoulder. The colors, of course, were red and white.

Two other girls, obviously with the speaker, stood on each side of the cheerleader. They were dressed in regular clothes, and both were very pretty as well.

Tears had immediately formed in Mary's eyes at the taunting words. She looked down at her plate. "My mom's not a whore."

The cheerleader crossed her arms. "Really." It was said more as a statement than a question. She leaned over the table, almost into Mary's face. "Then, please, tell us your father's name."

Mary said nothing. The tears had broken free, and were flowing down her cheeks. "Just go away, Teresa."

Teresa, the cheerleader, stood upright. "See? Just like I said. Whore."

Mary covered her face with her hands and began sobbing.

Carol Grace had been growing angrier and angrier at the exchange. She had been waiting for Mary to stand up to the cheerleader, but it appeared that Mary wasn't up to the task. Fear and shame were holding her back.

Carol Grace had seen girls like this one back in the city. They were quick to judge others when they felt that they were better than other people.

It made her angry then.

Today, it made her furious.

"Back off, you vain bitch," said Carol Grace quietly.

The cheerleader turned her attention to Carol Grace. Teresa, as Mary had called her, crossed her arms, raised her eyebrows, and moved her head back and forth as she said, "Why should I, new girl?"

"She's my friend," replied Carol Grace simply.

"And *you're* going to stick up for her? Oh, please!" The cheerleader leaned in close to Carol Grace. "Anybody that sticks up for a crack whore's daughter *must* be a whore herself. Tell me how much you charge, and I'll pass it along to the baseball team!"

Carol Grace, anger flaring in her eyes, looked into the cheerleader's eyes. "I wish your hair would fall out, your family would lose all of its money, and your ass would grow so big that it would *never* fit into that cheerleader dress!"

"Oh, *really!*" said the cheerleader, as she stood upright again. "Well, if wishes were horses, crack whore daughters would ride!" As she finished this sentence, she tossed her head, which caused her ponytail to flip in the air. But, the ponytail continued flying through the air, even after the girl's head had stopped. It landed in another girl's lunch two tables down. The rest of that table jumped out of their chairs with screams of "Ewww!" and "Gross!" The remaining hair on the cheerleader's head dropped to the ground slowly, as if they were snowflakes floating from the ceiling. She put her hands on her head, and screamed when she realized that her hair had mostly fallen out.

Carol Grace and Mary stared at this sudden change with surprised looks on their faces. They looked around and realized that everyone in the cafeteria was staring, too.

As everyone stared, a rubbery sound began, as if someone were inflating a balloon.

The cheerleader began screaming again. As everyone stared in wonder, the girl's hips and buttocks began growing larger...and larger...and larger. The width of her hips had easily doubled in size, and the cheerleader shorts underneath couldn't compete. They began splitting along the seams on either side, until they reached the taut strand of elastic at the top. The strap was stretched so tightly that it was obviously hurting the cheerleader, and cutting off circulation. She was saved from gangrene, or worse, when the strap snapped like a rubber band. The girl's buttocks swelled and grew outward until they looked like a huge exaggeration of what was commonly called a "bubble butt". The girl's underwear shredded along each seam, and the elastic top shared the same fate as the elastic from the cheerleader shorts. When her buttocks stopped expanding, the girl's butt stuck out a full twelve inches from her waistline.

People all across the cafeteria, faced with the outrageous growth of the cheerleader's hips and behind, teamed with the suddenly bald head, couldn't contain themselves. They began laughing uproariously at the absurdity of the sight.

But, the final humiliation for Teresa remained. Still screaming, she began running toward the cafeteria's exit. The cheerleader slipped on some food that someone had dropped, and her feet flew out from under her. She landed solidly...on her behind. As she tried to get back up, the girl found that the only way she could regain her feet was to rock back and forth on her bottom, until she could turn enough to get to her knees and stand up from there. She ran the rest of the way out the door.

Amid the cafeteria's laughter, Mary said to Carol Grace, "Do we have a magic genie or something?"

"I NEED SOME ARTILLERY, Bill," said Alan.

Alan and Billy were inside the sheriff's car, driving to Perry Guns And Ammo.

"That's where we're heading now," said Billy. "The owner of the gun shop is a firm believer in being prepared. He's a survivalist...but, he's a good man. He's level-headed, and he's not nuts on the subject. The difference with him is that he's always willing to help someone else. He should have lots of things to make things...difficult...for Moses Turley."

Alan nodded. "Sounds good." He hesitated. "She kissed me, Billy."

Billy smiled. "I saw that."

Alan shook his head. "I'm still having trouble believing it."

Billy shrugged. "I don't see a problem with it. She likes you, Alan...maybe she wants to be more than friends. Isn't that what you wanted since high school?"

"Yeah, but not this way, Bill," said Alan. "I don't want to put Katie or Carol Grace in danger. I'd rather let Turley kill me than to have either one of them hurt...or worse." He shook his head sadly. "A cop's work doesn't much allow for a personal life...or a family."

"Is that why you never married?"

Billy glanced at his friend. "You know the answer to that."

"Bill, it's been years. Phoebe may be a recovering alcholic and addict, but that's the point: she's *over* it!"

"Dammit, Alan! It was never the drinking or the partying! It was the *cheating!*"

"Billy, she swore that somebody put something in her beer at that party, and that she was raped. I believed her then, and I still believe her. You should, too, if you ever cared for her at all."

Billy didn't reply.

"You dumped her, man...and for no more reason than she was raped. How long have you been a cop? You should know all about rape, so how can you call it *cheating?* Even here, I'm sure rape comes up more than it should."

"Alan. Even if she *was* raped, why the drinking? The drugs?"

"Billy, she was raped, left pregnant, thrown out of her house by her parents, and dumped by the man she loved. She probably felt like nobody cared...like all she was good for was some scumbag's good time. What would *you* do in that situation?" Alan shook his head. "All I'm saying is that you should consider a second chance, man. Love doesn't grow on trees, but you still have to feed it to make it grow. She deserves that, Bill...just like *you* deserve the chance to ask her to forgive you."

After a moment, Billy said, "Katie doesn't know any of that, does she?"

Alan shook his head. "No. Unless Phoebe told her, and I doubt that happened. All she knows is that Phoebe still cares about you. And Carol Grace is...well, let's just say that she's being forced to spend time with Mary."

Billy laughed. "What happened?"

Alan told Billy the story of the lunchroom fight between Carol Grace and Mary. He then told Billy about the first time he met Carol Grace. By the time he was finished, both men were laughing.

"Wow," said Billy, shaking his head and laughing. "The kid's a spitfire, all right."

"She doesn't back down, that's for sure. I'm finding out that Katie's the same way."

"Alan, old buddy, if Katie's anything like she was in high school, you ain't seen nothin' yet."

Billy turned the car into the parking lot of Perry Guns And Ammo.

"Let's go shopping," said Billy, as the men got out of the car.

THE GREETING THAT KATIE received as she reached the end of the driveway in front of the farmhouse wasn't what she expected.

Margo Sardis was seated on the front porch, in the same rocking chair that she had used the previous night.

Katie smiled in spite of her misgivings. This *was* her aunt, after all.

Katie climbed out of the car and waved. "Hi, Aunt Margo!"

"Hello, child."

Katie went to the bottom of the steps. "Will you be okay for a few minutes, Aunt Margo? I have chickens and feed in the car, and I need to get those chicks safely into the coop."

Margo chuckled. "Let me help you with that, Katie."

"Are you sure it's no trouble? The chicks don't weigh a lot, but the feed bags are fifty pounders."

"Well, I sure won't turn down any help! Let me grab one of the feed bags, and..." She didn't finish the sentence.

Margo dropped her head down, as if praying, and was muttering words that Katie couldn't hear. Margo then lifted her cane, and kept it at a right angle as she pointed her arm toward the car. A blue bolt of energy flashed from the top of the cane, enveloped the car, then disappeared. So did the chicks and bags of feed.

"All done, niece," said Margo calmly. "Chicks are fed, watered, and safely under the heat lamps. And the feed is put away."

Katie could only stare at the car, trying to believe what she had just seen.

"Katie, cat gotcher tongue?" asked Margo.

Katie nodded. "Was that...did you...I don't..."

Margo nodded. "Yes, Katie. That was magic, I did it, and I know you don't...but I'm here to teach you."

A BLACK MERCEDES SEDAN sped along the Interstate highway, heading for the Sardis County exit. Four men rode inside, two in front and two in back.

One of the men in the back was Moses Turley. The others were the men arrested with Turley. They had been riding for an hour.

Finally, the man in the front passenger seat spoke. "Hey, Mose, do we know where this cop is?"

Turley shook his head. "No. All Rizzo got from the other cop was that Blake could possibly be in Sardis County. He said that Blake grew up there."

"His parents still there, or somethin'?"

"Cop's parents are dead, Tolani," replied Turley.

The other two men, Joe Flore and Gino Blasi, were silent as Turley and Tolani talked.

"He got any other relatives?" asked Tolani.

"No," said Turley.

A couple of moments passed.

"So, what you're sayin' is that we don't know if the cop's even *in* Sardis County?" ventured Tolani.

"That's right, Tolani," answered Turley.

Another short pause...then Tolani said, "Mose, if we don't know he's there, why we goin'?"

Turley exploded, and smacked Tolani on the back of the head with a newspaper. "Holy Mary Mother-of-*God*, Tolani! We're going for two reasons! One, he *might* be there, and, if he is, we're gonna take him out! Two, Rizzo and Mickey Giambini *told* us to go, you fucking moron!"

Tolani had ducked when Turley smacked the back of his head, and was now silent.

Several minutes went by.

Finally, Tolani broke the silence. "We gonna get a motel room, Mose?"

Turley took a deep breath before answering, trying to calm himself. "No, we're gonna find the dirtiest, filthiest, hog farm there, and we're gonna sleep in the mud with the pigs! Of *course* we're gonna get a motel room!" Turley took another deep breath. "We're staying in Perry. We'll be strangers there, so we gotta be careful. I'll give each one of you a picture of Blake, then we'll start asking around. Somebody will have seen him, if he's there. Might take a few days, but, if he's there, we'll find him."

The car sped down the highway quietly for several minutes.

"Hey, Mose?" said Tolani.

Turley put his hand over his eyes. "*What,* Tolani?"

"Hey, you through with that newspaper?"

Turley hit the back of Tolani's head with the newspaper several times, then threw the tattered remains into the front seat.

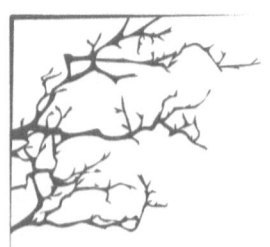

Chapter 9

Carol Grace and Mary made only one more wish that day. They wished that the cheerleader went back to normal. After that, they decided to wait until they could talk about it freely, and they couldn't do that in school.

School released each day at two-thirty in the afternoon. At two-thirty, Ms. Buckner released the girls.

"I hope you have a good evening, girls," Buckner said. "You've done well today. I'll see you tomorrow."

As soon as the girls went into the hallway, they began chatting.

"So, why don't we call our moms right now?" said Carol Grace. "You'll be able to come home with me on the bus Friday afternoon!"

Mary shook her head. "I can't. Mom's at work at Mackie's right now. I can't call her unless it's an emergency. She gets off at six. I'll ask her then, and I'll call you tonight."

They had reached the door leading outside to the school buses. Impulsively, Carol Grace hugged Mary tightly.

"Mary, I'm so sorry about what happened before."

"So am I, Carol Grace. But, that's over now!"

Carol Grace smiled at her new friend. "Talk to you tonight!"

"Sounds good!"

The girls each went to their assigned bus for the ride home.

"HOLY CRAP, ALAN! YOU really hit the jackpot!"

Alan and Billy were walking back to the sheriff's car. Both men were loaded down with all they could carry: two rifles, three shotguns, three revolvers, several boxes of ammunition, four cans of pepper spray, a couple of police-style tasers, some flash grenades, and other odds and ends. The artillery had cost Alan a fortune, but it had all been worth it.

Alan's next step worried him. He had to convince Katie that not only were these items necessary, but that she and Carol Grace had to learn how to use all of them, if they didn't know already. He would teach them not only *how* to shoot, but also something else that was just as important: *when* to shoot.

"Billy, I may need your help convincing Katie that all of this is necessary."

Billy smiled. "No problem, Alan. She'll listen."

"Thank you. That would be great. If something happened to her or Carol Grace because of me, I don't think I could ever forgive myself."

"*Concentrate,* Katie," said Margo. "The words are a big part of making a spell, but the power is inside you, and you have to concentrate to make it work. Now, try it again."

"Yes, ma'am," said Katie.

Margo had taught Katie the same protection spell from the night before, so that Katie could renew it every night. Now, she was teaching Katie a new spell...one to get the fields plowed and ready for planting. It was much more difficult than Katie had anticipated.

Katie *could* feel the power inside herself, and it seemed overwhelming. The power, however wasn't the problem. Focusing her *control* of the power was going to take a lot of practice.

"Picture what you want to happen, until that's all you can see in your mind, then let the power go," said Margo calmly and quietly. "What you picture happening becomes reality."

Katie focused. She pictured the fields plowed, tilled, and ready for planting. She concentrated until that was all that she could see in her mind, then she released the power. It flowed from inside her, and to the end of her arm, becoming a pale blue light that glowed with intense purpose. She felt the power leaving her, and spreading through all of the fields, making her command a reality. She opened her mind, and saw that the fields were complete, down to the last ounce of fertilizer. Katie backed the power back down inside herself.

When the power was tamped down and calm, Katie sighed heavily, and sank into the rocking chair on the front porch. Little Bit was between the two women, head on her paws, fast asleep. She smiled despite herself. Only a short while ago, she didn't even believe in magic.

"Aunt Margo, that was exhilarating! Exhilarating and exhausting!"

Margo smiled at her niece. "I'm sure it was, Katie. I remember the first big spell that I ever did – I felt tired for two days!"

The two women sat quietly on the front porch for a time. Katie was amazed at how quickly she had wrapped her mind around the fact that, not only was she a Sardis, but a witch, too!

A question popped into Katie's mind, and she asked it. "Aunt Margo, what about Carol Grace? Does she have power inside her, too?"

Margo was silent, staring out at the fields. Just as Katie started to ask the question again, Margo answered. "Probably, but I can't be sure." She looked at Katie. "I'm afraid that the power may be weakening as it descends the ancestral line. We'll find out, though. Right now, we're working on you."

Katie nodded.

"Now, don't forget to do that protection spell tonight, Katie," reminded Margo.

"Aunt Margo, why is that spell so important?" asked Katie.

At first, Katie didn't think that Margo would answer. Margo stared out over the fields, glancing here and there, until she finally looked down at the porch. "Katie, the spell is for protection against certain...things...that may be roaming around."

"Things?" Katie asked tentatively.

Margo nodded, then nodded again as if she had made a decision. "A short while ago, I'm ashamed to say that I sold a man a summoning spell."

"Go on, Aunt Margo."

"Patience, child, I'm not proud of what I did," retorted Margo. "It's hard to talk about, but it's a good thing for you to know. I don't want you to make the same mistake." She looked into Katie's eyes. "Do you remember what I said about giving people exactly what they ask for?"

Katie nodded. "Yes, ma'am."

"Then forget it! I was wrong!" said Margo vehemently. "A short while ago, a man named Ricky Jackson came to me for a summoning spell. I knew that he wanted it to summon the spirit of his dead wife, but *he didn't say that*. He only asked for a summoning spell." Margo paused. "I used to be young once, you know."

"Of course you were, Aunt Margo."

"Oh, Katie, it was so long ago...and time, thieving time, comes in the night and steals away the years! But the heart, child...the heart knows what it wants, and, years ago, mine wanted Ricky Jackson." A small tear sprang from Margo's eye, and slid quietly, almost cautiously, down the old witch's cheek. "But, he fell in love with another, and married her. And I was jealous! I was so eaten with jealousy that I caught myself working up a spell that would literally kill them both! But, somehow, I calmed down and stopped. I figured that their union wouldn't last long, and, when it ended, Ricky would come to me. But, time came creeping along and stole the years, and their marriage continued...and continued. She passed away a couple of short years ago, and Ricky recently came to me for the summoning spell." Margo sniffed, and wiped her hand across her cheek. "And, God help me, I gave it to him."

"What happened?" asked Katie quietly.

Margo didn't say anything for a long moment. "The spell I gave him was a general summoning spell. It worked better than I expected. Ricky summoned a Hellhound."

Katie's eyes widened.

"It couldn't kill him, because it couldn't get to him," continued Margo. "It was contained within a pentagram for several months, because Ricky didn't know how to get rid of it. Then, one day, some high school kids came along to Ricky's to do some free work on his property. They accidentally released the Hellhound, and it killed one of them. The other two kids, and Ricky, showed up at my place for help." Margo paused again. "The Hellhound was summoned through a doorway to Hell. Once the hound was loose, the doorway was open and unattended. Some adventurous residents of that side of reality took advantage of the opportunity, and came over to Sardis County before I got the doorway shut again." Margo sighed deeply. "The kids killed the Hellhound, and saved us...but Ricky's disappeared. I think something got him." Margo's haunted stare met Katie's wonder-filled eyes. "That's what the protection spell is for, Katie...the things that came through are still in Sardis County. And I don't know what they are, or where they are...but, I don't want them to focus in on me...or you." She leaned forward and took Katie's hand in hers. "I don't want anyone else I love hurt by my own stupid vanity."

Katie, unsure what to say, merely squeezed her aunt's hand...but, in consideration of Margo's age, not *too* tightly.

"How many came across, do you think?" asked Katie.

Margo shook her head. "I have no idea, child. That scares me."

The sound of Mary McKinnon's school bus trundling along the road came to them.

"Oh, it's Carol Grace!" exclaimed Katie. "Is it that late already? Aunt Margo, I'm so glad that you're finally getting a chance to meet her!"

"So am I, sweet niece. So am I." Margo smiled.

"She's really going to be surprised!" said Katie. *But maybe not* too *surprised.*

ALAN AND BILLY WERE in the sheriff's car, following Mary McKinnon's bus along the road. When it stopped and released Carol Grace, Alan yelled through the open passenger window.

"Hey, kid! Get in the car! You're under arrest!"

Carol Grace giggled at the two men and trotted to the car. "Hi, Alan! Hi, Billy! What's up?"

"Just getting back, Carol Grace. We've been running errands. Hop in. We'll drive you to the house...save you a few steps."

Carol Grace opened the car's back door and climbed in. After the door had shut, she said, "Hey! There's no door handle back here!"

The two men chuckled as Billy turned into the driveway.

"Guess I'll have to haul you to jail," said Billy.

Carol Grace sniffed, then wrinkled her nose. "Ewww...it *stinks* back here! It smells like...like somebody *puked!*"

Both men burst out laughing as Carol Grace put her hand over her nose.

"Hurry *up* and let me out of here!" cried the teen.

"Hey, Alan, check out the front porch," said Billy, as he parked the car.

Alan looked up. Katie was sitting with an old woman. Realization hit him, and he blurted, "Margo Sardis!"

"Who's Margo Sardis?" asked Carol Grace. "And open the door! *Please!*"

The men climbed out of the car, and Billy opened the back door. Carol Grace came tumbling out, retching slightly.

"Oh, my *God*, I never want to ride back there again!" she said as led the way to the porch. To her mother, she said, "Hi, Mom! Can Mary Smalls spend the night Friday night?" Then she noticed the other woman on the porch. "I'm sorry! Hi, Miz Sardis."

Margo smiled. "You know who I am, Carol Grace?"

Carol Grace nodded. "At least, I know who Billy and Alan said you were."

Margo chuckled. "Hello, Sheriff Napier."

Billy nodded and said, "Miz Sardis."

Margo turned to Alan. "You must be the young man that Katie seems so smitten with."

Smitten with? Alan's mind whirled with the information.

Katie blushed.

"Cat got your tongue, son?" asked Margo gently.

Alan snapped back into reality. "I'm sorry, Miz Sardis. I'm Alan Blake."

Margo offered her hand to Alan, and he shook it gently. "Back home from the big, bad city, I see."

Margo turned to Carol Grace.

"Carol Grace. It's nice to meet you, child," said Margo.

"It's nice to meet you, ma'am," replied Carol Grace.

Alan had pulled chairs around for all of them. They all sat and rocked.

Katie said, "Sweetie, Margo is your aunt." She continued, explaining their relationship to Margo.

"So, we're descended from the people that this county is named for?" asked Carol Grace excitedly. "That is so *cool!*" The teen hugged her mother, then hugged Margo. Little Bit jumped around the girl, barking happily. "I'm a *Sardis!* Woo-hoo!"

Carol Grace's smile was contagious. Katie found herself laughing at her daughter's excitement, both men were smiling, and even Margo had a small smile on her face.

"Good grief, Carol Grace!" said Katie, laughing. "Don't hold back! Let us know how you *really* feel!"

Everyone chuckled at Katie's joke.

"Hey, Mom! Can we change our names to 'Sardis'?" asked Carol Grace excitedly.

"Of *course* not, silly!" replied Katie.

After more chatting and laughing, Katie made an announcement.

"Saturday evening. I want all of you here. We're grilling out...burgers, probably, and maybe some hot dogs. Baked beans, cole slaw, homemade French fries...all will be on the menu. We'll all just enjoy ourselves and have fun just hanging out. We'll start around six o'clock, if Alan will kindly do the grilling honors."

Alan smiled at Katie. "I'd be honored."

"Billy? Aunt Margo?"

"I'll be here," said Billy. "I never pass up free food. But, I'll bring some drinks along to pay my way."

Katie smiled at her old friend. "Not necessary, but accepted. Aunt Margo, please say you'll be here."

Margo smiled, and nodded. "I'll be here, child. Thank you."

"Hey, mom, what about..." began Carol Grace.

Katie cut her off with widened eyes and a slight shake of the head.

Carol Grace, puzzled, kept quiet.

Finally, Alan said, "Katie, I have something I need to talk to you about."

"Before you do, may I make a suggestion, Alan?" replied Katie.

"Sure."

"I think we need to think about buying a couple of rifles and shotguns for protection from those criminals you're trying to avoid. If they find out that you're here, we'll need something to defend ourselves with. Grampy's old shotgun and rifle are antiques, and I'd really rather not fire them with modern ammunition."

Alan, caught by surprise, was speechless. After a moment, Billy burst out laughing.

"What did I tell you, Alan?" said Billy, laughing. "I told you that she might surprise you!"

Katie, smiling but not understanding, asked, "What's so funny?"

Alan explained what he and Billy had been doing that day, and his plans to give shooting lessons to Katie and Carol Grace.

"Wow!" said Carol Grace. "I can shoot better than Mom!"

"Once! One time!" exclaimed Katie.

Carol Grace, smiling, began taunting her mother. "I shot better than you-u! I shot better than you-u!"

"Brat!" said Katie, smiling.

Billy slapped his hands on his knees and stood up. "Well, Alan, I'll give you a hand unloading your weaponry, then I'll have to get back to town."

"Sure, Billy," said Alan, as he stood. He glanced around as he headed for the steps, then stopped. His eyes were wide.

Katie, concerned, said, "Alan, what's wrong?"

"The fields...they're all plowed and ready...how...when...?"

Katie ducked her head. Margo started laughing.

"Go unload your guns, Alan, and then I'll tell you all about it," replied Katie.

"Katie, I need to be going, too," said Margo.

"Do you have to, Aunt Margo?" asked Carol Grace.

"I'm sorry, little one, but I have to."

"But I'll see you on Saturday, right?"

"Little one, I wouldn't miss it for the world," replied Margo.

The old witch stood. She turned to Billy.

"Think you could give an old woman a ride to town, Sheriff?" Margo asked.

"I believe I can find some room for you, ma'am."

Margo hugged her nieces, then held her hand out to Alan.

When Alan took Margo's hand, he felt a jolt move through his arm. It travelled all through his body, then went back through his arm to Margo. His wide eyes met hers.

"Just what the hell was that?" asked Alan, still holding the old woman's hand.

"Checking you out. Seeing if you're good enough for my niece."

Alan gave a half smile. "And did I pass?"

Margo met his gaze. "You did. Your love for her is almost as deep as her love for you. And you'll take good care of her and Carol Grace." Her gaze turned stern. "You'd better...or you'll have me to answer to. You'll also need to get rid of that trouble you brought from the city. But, not to worry. It will come to a head soon." She released Alan's hand and turned to Katie. "Child, you also will need to be strong for him, and take care of him. Trust in him, and in his judgements.

He's wiser than you know. Most of all, show him that you love him." She then turned to Carol Grace. "As for you, little one...respect this man. He'd gladly die for you, if need be...and it may yet happen. Pay attention, and do what you can to help your family."

Carol Grace looked both frightened and solemn. "Yes, Aunt Margo."

"I've said enough. Time to go to town, if the High Sheriff is ready!"

Billy snapped off a salute. "Yes, *ma'am!*"

"No need to be a smartass, young man," said Margo.

"Yes, ma'am."

Billy opened the car door for the old woman.

"Thank you, Billy," said Margo.

"You're welcome, ma'am." To the three people on the porch, Billy said, "I'll see you folks around six on Saturday."

Alan waved. "See you then, Bill!"

As the sheriff's car drove along the driveway to the road, Alan casually slipped his arm around Katie's waist. Carol Grace noticed, then smiled.

Katie felt a pleasant heat running throughout her body as Alan put his arm around her. Inside, she was melting, and her heart was tripping along at super speed. *His arm feels like...like it should have been there all along! Oh, Mark, I've fallen in love again! I know you want me to be happy, and I also know you'll forgive me.*

Alan was enjoying the feel of Katie's firm waist under his hand and arm. It was arousing him like no other woman's touch ever had. *It's true! There's one woman for every man, and I've found mine. Dear God, please let me spend the rest of my life with this woman!*

"Alan and Kat-ie, sitting in a tree..." sang Carol Grace tauntingly.

Alan burst out laughing, and Katie smiled. "All right, young lady, enough of that!"

Carol Grace giggled.

"Now, since Billy isn't here right now, what was that about Mary Smalls?" asked Katie.

Remembrance showed on Carol Grace's face. "Oh, yeah! Can Mary spend the night on Friday night?"

Katie turned away from Alan's arm...reluctantly...toward Carol Grace, and put her hands on her hips. "What? Just yesterday, you were saying that spending time with Mary would be torture!"

Carol Grace grinned. "I know. But, she's pretty cool. I like her a lot!"

"Now, see? I was right, wasn't I?"

"Yes, you were! So can she spend the night Friday?"

"Think you can stand two teen girls running around the farm Friday night, Alan?" asked Katie.

"The more, the merrier," said Alan cheerfully.

"Really? Yay!" exclaimed Carol Grace.

"Have you cleared it with Phoebe yet?" asked Katie.

Carol Grace shook her head. "No, Mary said that her mom had to work until six tonight. She'll ask her then."

"Tell you what...why don't I call tonight? I need to talk to Phoebe anyway."

"Okay...but I still want to talk to Mary, all right?"

Katie smiled. "Yes, honey." Suddenly, she remembered something. "There are chickens in the chicken house, if you want to go check them out."

Excitement bubbled over again from Carol Grace. "*Really?* We have *chickens?* Come on, Little Bit!" Carol Grace began running to the end of the porch, then leaped off, heading in the direction of the chicken house.

"Wow," said Katie. She turned to Alan. "Okay, I know you have questions."

Alan shook his head. "No...no, I don't have any."

Katie looked sideways at him. "Not even about the fields?"

Alan shook his head again. "Nope. I already know the answer."

Katie put her hands on her hips. "Okay, Mr. Smart Guy, what's the answer?"

"Well, if your Aunt Margo is a witch, and you're a Sardis, that must mean you're a witch, too."

Katie's mouth hung open. "How in the *world* did you figure that out?"

Alan smiled smugly. "Hey, I *am* a good detective...remember?"

AT THE PERRY MOTOR Court, Moses Turley and his men had just checked into two rooms on the end. Each room had two beds.

Turley told the men to freshen up, and meet back in the room he was sharing with Joe Flore. He had assigned Gino Blasi to bunk with Tolani.

Turley was afraid that he'd beat Tolani to death if he had to share a room with him.

When the men met in Turley's room, Turley handed each man a photograph of Alan Blake.

"Here's what we're gonna do," he said. "We'll wander around town, asking if anybody knows this guy, Alan Blake. You're all in town on business with your boss, and Blake is an old college friend of your boss. You wanna surprise both your boss and Blake by hooking them up again after all these years, and do they know him, have they seen him, and so on. If Blake's here, somebody has seen him...and people love to talk."

"What do they love to talk about, Mose?" asked Tolani.

Turley slowly turned his head to Tolani. His entire face was deadpan as he said, "They love to talk about what a saint I am *FOR PUTTIN' UP WITH A FUCKIN' RETARD LIKE YOU!*"

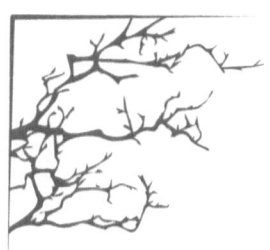

Chapter 10

"You know, Sheriff, you ought to offer a deputy job to Alan," said Margo. Margo and Billy Napier were driving to town, having just left Junior's Farm.

"He's got a job in the city, Miz Sardis."

"He'll want another, just to keep busy. The farm will mostly take care of itself, and he'll get bored."

Billy smirked. "Now, what makes you think he'll be around Sardis County?"

"He's so in love with Katie, he couldn't bear to go back to the city."

They rode in silence for a couple of miles.

"You know, Miz Sardis, I just might do that. It would be nice to have Alan back home. And I could sure use the help. That moron that the Perry City Council gave the Chief Of Police job to...well, let's just say that if trouble raised its head around him, Chief Godfrey Malcolm would disappear faster than a fart in a high wind. If he wasn't too drunk to stand up," he added.

Margo chuckled at this analogy. But, she couldn't fault Billy's judgment of the man.

"Where can I drop you off, Miz Sardis?"

"Mackie's, please, if it's no trouble. I have to pick up a few things."

"Will you be able to get home okay?"

Margo smiled. "Yes, I will, Sheriff. Thank you for askin'."

"SO, BASICALLY, WE'RE ambushing Billy," said Alan.

Katie smiled. "Yes, we are. Katie's plan to have Mary spend the night with us on Friday fits right in. Phoebe will be here to pick up Mary, and Billy will be here, too...maybe the sparks can fly."

Alan looked at his hands. "Did you know that Billy and Phoebe were together for a while back in high school?"

Katie's eyes widened. "That's right! I'd forgotten all about that!" She stared out at the fields, forming her next question. "I know they split up pretty quickly, but I never did know why. Do you?"

Alan shook his head. "Katie, please don't ask me that. It isn't my story to tell, and I don't want to betray any confidences."

Katie nodded her understanding. "Fair enough. My nefarious plot is to take Phoebe out Saturday and get her all dolled up...hair fixed, makeup done, new outfit...I'm going to make sure she goes all out! And maybe...just maybe, mind you...Billy will take a second look."

"And a second chance. If anyone can do it, you can, Katie."

"Thank you, sir." Katie took a deep breath. "Okay, Alan, I know you have questions about the witch thing. Ask away."

"Actually, I don't," replied Alan. "You told me all about the visit from Margo Sardis the other night, so I know when you found out. And the results are obvious." He paused, and looked out over the fields for a few seconds. "What about planting? Won't people be suspicious if we don't buy seed?"

Katie smiled. "Aunt Margo said that we had to buy seed. I can't conjure it up out of thin air. She also said that I could plant them myself, and that she would help me work through the spell."

Alan nodded. "Good enough, then. I don't have anything else." He chuckled. "It's amazing what I can accept on short notice."

Katie chuckled at his remark. She glanced at Alan's profile. *His eyes are everywhere, and I bet he doesn't even know it! Always on the lookout for trouble!* She decided to take a longer look, and turned her head to Alan, studying him. If he noticed as he rocked in his chair, he didn't let on. *Mark, forgive me. I will always love you, but you're gone. I've fallen in love with this man, and I want to believe that you'd want me to be happy again.*

"Alan," began Katie shyly, "can we talk about...us?"

Alan stopped rocking briefly, then started again. Cautiously, he replied, "What about us, Katie?" *Here it comes...she's going to dump me! Watch, you dumb cop: here's your hopes, going right down the drain!*

Slowly, Katie said, "*Is* there an 'us'?"

Alan's heart leapt into his throat. His head turned toward Katie so quickly that it made a popping sound. He took her hand into his, looked into her eyes, and said intensely, "Katie Ballantine Montgomery, there is an 'us' for the rest of my pitiful life, if you want it."

Katie's eyes widened with realization. "Oh, I want it, Alan!" she said, as she threw her arms around him. He did the same, and they hugged each other tightly, fiercely, from their sitting position. Then, their lips found each other. The kiss was long and intense. Everything else was lost as their lips expressed their desires, and their tongues met, first tentatively, then with more passion. No passage of time intruded on this moment, no thoughts went through their minds...except of happiness and desire.

"Ewww, *gross!*" said Carol Grace as she rounded the corner of the house with Little Bit. "Do you have to muah right on the front *porch?*"

Katie and Alan burst out laughing, breaking the kiss.

The teenager climbed the front steps, talking all the way. "I mean, really, if you two are going to muah all over each other, take it in*side,* please! PDAs are a little bit TMI, you know?"

"Hey, kid," said Alan.

"What, you mack?" said Carol Grace mockingly.

"Shut your cake-hole. Go do your homework."

Katie and Alan started laughing. After a moment, so did Carol Grace.

When Carol Grace stopped laughing, she looked from her mother to Alan, and back. "So, are you two a unit now?"

Katie's smile played around the edges of her mouth. "I suppose we are. Is that okay with you, Carol Grace?"

The teenager eyed Alan closely. "Well...I guess he's not *totally* disgusting...," and started running down the steps, laughing. Alan chased her around the yard, with Little Bit running with the two, barking excitedly.

Katie watched the three of them bouncing around the yard, and smiled broadly. She found that she was *very* happy.

MOSES TURLEY WAS NOT happy.

As the afternoon wore away to evening, and evening turned into the dinner hour, Turley and his group hadn't had the tiniest nibble on the whereabouts of Alan Blake.

Turley was beginning to wonder if Blake really was in Sardis County.

Moses Turley wasn't an idiot. He knew that he had only a very slight chance of remaining alive after this "arrested" fiasco, and that chance depended on finding Alan Blake, killing him, and then finding somewhere to lay low.

Turley knew that after he killed Blake, there wouldn't be any "high life" for him...he'd have to live the "low" life in order to keep living at all. Mickey Giambini didn't forgive mistakes easily, and getting arrested by a couple of undercover cops was one of the biggest mistakes a guy in his line of work could make. But, if it all blew over because no witnesses could be found, Mickey *might*...just *might*...let Turley live.

Turley didn't count on it, however. He'd seen too many of Mickey's people come and go...and go in the worst possible way. Their mistakes hadn't been as bad as Turley's, so he could see the writing on the Giambini wall.

Turley had a rabbit hole prepared, with plenty of money to keep him happy. It was in South America, far away from the city...and the Giambini family.

But, tonight he had to eat...and so did his men. Turley was driving past a store, and decided to pull into the parking lot. He would prepare spaghetti tonight, with his private recipe sauce. Maybe some garlic bread. The motel room had a kitchenette with a refrigerator, microwave, and hot plate. He could do it, if he could get the right ingredients.

As he walked into the store, Turley glanced up at the sign. *Mackie's. Great. Probably named after some haggis-eating, kilt-wearing Scotsman. Good luck finding good Italian ingredients.* Once inside, however, he found everything he needed to complete the evening's menu. He carried his purchases to the checkout line.

The old woman in front of him was chatting with the cashier. The cashier was pretty, but Turley could spot an alcoholic from a mile away. Maybe she was recovering, but she definitely was an alcoholic. That thought led him to memories of the past, filled with drunken men that wagered everything on the turn of a card...usually to Turley's benefit. He came quickly back to reality when he tuned in to the women's conversation, and a name clicked inside his head.

"Phoebe, that Alan Blake is just the man for Katie," said the old woman to the cashier. "He'll make a good stepfather to Carol Grace, too."

"I think so, too, Miss Margo," replied the cashier.

"Now, you be ready, you hear? Katie is going to call you tonight, to ask if Mary can spend the night Friday night. Then, there's going to be a small cookout Saturday evening. Alan's gonna be the chef...outside, anyway!" The old woman cackled, then tightened her grip on her cane. "And don't forget to make sure that you're off on Saturday! You've got to be able to come to Junior's Farm!"

The cashier smiled at the old woman. "I'll make sure before I leave tonight, Miss Margo. You take care now!"

The old woman walked away from the checkout line, with her cane in one hand, and a small plastic bag in the other.

Turley placed his items on the conveyor belt and smiled at the cashier. "I'm sorry, but I couldn't help but overhear part of your conversation. Did one of you mention an Alan Blake?"

The cashier was concentrating on ringing up the items that Turley was purchasing. She seemed distracted when she answered. "Sure did. He's an old schoolmate of mine."

Turley, playing his part, said, "I know an Alan Blake in the city. He's a cop. That couldn't be the same man."

"Oh, yes, that's Alan!" She looked at Turley. "How do you know him?" she asked suspiciously, as if Turley was a criminal. He was, but he surely couldn't let this dimwit know.

Instead, he laughed. "I handle his his automobile insurance. I'm trying to get him to buy some renter's insurance, but he's a tough man to convince!"

Relief showed in the cashier's face. "That's Alan, all right. He always was stubborn, once his mind was made up. Are you in town to visit him?" she asked, as she counted out Turley's change.

"No, I'm here to help another agent," said Turley, the lie passing his lips with little effort. "I had no idea Alan was in Sardis County. Since he is, I may try to say 'hello' to him. Is he staying in town?"

The cashier shook her head. "He's staying with a lady named Katie Montgomery, out on Junior's Farm." She gave him rudimentary directions.

"Thank you so much," said Turley.

"You're welcome. Come back and see us!" The cashier began ringing up the next person in line.

Turley resisted the urge to run back to the car. But he didn't resist the urge to grin from ear to ear.

Turley didn't notice that the old woman that had been ahead of him in line was now standing off to the side of the entrance. She had a small smile on her face as she watched Turley drive away.

Margo Sardis figured that the sooner this bad thing was dealt with, the better Katie would be. She was still smiling as she faded from sight, heading home.

KATIE CALLED PHOEBE around seven that evening...sort of. Carol Grace actually did the calling, and it was Mary that Carol Grace called. After the girls chatted excitedly for a few minutes, Carol Grace told Mary that Katie wanted to talk to Phoebe, and the phone was passed on both ends.

"Hello?" asked Phoebe.

"Hi, Phoebe, this is Katie."

"Oh, hi, Katie! Miss Margo told me that you would call tonight!"

"Oh, did she? Did she mention why?"

"She told me that the girls had plans to stay with you on Friday night, and that there was a cookout at your place Saturday evening."

Katie laughed. "That's Aunt Margo for you. She jumped the gun, but that's great!"

"*Aunt* Margo?" asked Phoebe.

"Oh, that's right! You don't know either! Phoebe, you're going to be as surprised as I am when I tell you, but..." Katie told Phoebe about the Sardis family connection.

"Wow, Katie! You're a Sardis! And you didn't know it?"

Katie shook her head as she spoke. "I never had a clue, Phoebe. But, it's nice knowing something about where I come from...and it's nice knowing that I still have a living older relative."

"I guess it is! Wow!"

"Listen, Phoebe, I have something up my sleeve, if you're interested."

"I'm all ears."

"Do you still want another chance with Billy?"

Phoebe was silent for so long that Katie thought she had disconnected the call.

"Phoebe?"

"I'm here."

"I hope I didn't overstep my bounds."

"No. Not at all." Phoebe paused, then continued. "Katie, I'd give almost anything for another chance with him."

Katie smiled. "Phoebe, you don't have to give up anything. As a matter of fact, it's all on me. I have a plan!"

"Then *share* it, Katie!"

"Okay, here's the deal, Phoebe, and you're not allowed to argue with me. First, I'm going to make appointments for both of us at Perry's best salon. We're getting our hair styled. And we're also getting manicures, pedicures, and makeovers. Then, we're going shopping. I'm going to find us the most attractive, flirtatious outfits all the way down to our shoes! Saturday night, Billy is coming to the farm for the cookout, along with Aunt Margo...but he *doesn't* know you're going to be there!"

"Katie, I can't afford all of that!"

"It doesn't matter, Phoebe. I can, and I'm going to. We're going fishing for two wonderful men, and we're the bait!"

MOSES TURLEY BURST into the men's motel room. Tolani had his sleeves rolled up, and was putting a couple of pots onto the hot plate. Flore and Blasi were sitting on the edges of the two beds, watching TV. When Turley burst into the room, all three of the men reached for the guns in their shoulder holsters, and relaxed when they saw it was Turley.

"Men, I know where Blake is hiding!" Turley slammed the door behind him, then stood straight, with a wide smile and his arms crossed. "All you gotta do is take me down to Junior's Farm!"

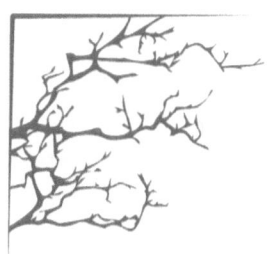

Chapter 11

Later that night, Carol Grace had yawned and said, "Good night!" She hugged Katie, and then hugged Alan.

"Might as well get started now," Carol Grace told them. "I have a feeling I'll be giving Alan 'good night' hugs for a looong time." The teen picked up Little Bit and went to her room.

"Alan, would you like to sit on the porch for a while?" asked Katie.

"I'd love it," Alan replied.

On the porch, under the starlight, Alan and Katie held hands, rocking chairs rocking with a slow, steady rhythm. Suddenly, Katie jumped up from her chair.

"Oh, no, I almost forgot!" exclaimed Katie.

Alan had stood, too. "Forgot what?"

"Aunt Margo taught me a protection spell the first night she was here. She told me to do it every night, to keep us safe from...well, I'll explain in a minute."

Katie closed her eyes and focused her energy. Alan watched closely, with a bemused look on his face.

Alan's face changed as Katie repeated the words of the protection spell. To Alan, the words sounded like both gibberish and a language that he almost understood.

Katie raised her right hand and pointed her index finger out at nothing in particular. A ball of blue power appeared from inside her, becoming brighter as it traveled from her back, to her shoulder, and then down her arm. As it reached her pointing finger, the ball was at its brightest. It leapt from her finger and spread out across the property, dimming again, then disappearing as it settled domelike over Junior's Farm.

Alan's mouth formed the word, "Wow", but no sound came from it. It remained open after forming the word.

Katie, smiling, reached over and gently closed Alan's mouth. "It's a protection spell. I have to use it every night. Aunt Margo sold a man a summoning spell in a fit of jealousy. The spell summoned a Hellhound...and left a doorway to Hell open. She said that she has no idea how many creatures crossed over through the open doorway, but they'd be attracted to the magic on Junior's Farm. The protection spell keeps them away."

"I...I know you told me," Alan said slowly. "And I believed you. I've seen the results." He shook his head. "I just never expected it to be so..."

"So ugly? So scary?" Katie was beginning to become defensive.

Alan shook his head to her questions. "No, Katie...so beautiful, so...so dazzling!" He took her hand in his, deliberately taking the hand that the power had just left, and looked into her eyes. "I'm so overwhelmed! It's one thing to believe in something, it's another thing to see it in action...and it's *wonderful!*" He wrapped his free arm around her waist and pulled her closely to him, laughing. "Dance with me, you amazing woman!" They began twirling around the porch, laughing, dancing, and enjoying each other's company. As they danced, they looked into each other's eyes, and both smiled.

As their lips touched, Katie and Alan lost all track of time. As their tongues touched briefly, then more passionately, they became consumed by each other.

Alan broke the kiss and the embrace. He held Katie by the shoulders and looked into her eyes. He was breathing heavily.

"Katie, I have to stop now."

With deep desire, Katie said, "Why?"

"If we keep this up, we'll wind up in either your bed or mine."

"And what's wrong with that, Alan? You know I want you." Katie looked down at the rise in Alan's jeans. "It's obvious that you want me, too," she said with a sultry laugh.

"It's too soon," Alan said simply. "I don't want this relationship to be based on sex. I want it to last forever, Katie."

Katie threw herself into Alan's arms. "If you say so, Alan. I guess you're right. But, it's been so long...so very long! And you have my heart in your hands."

Alan buried his face in Katie's hair as he held her tight. "I know, and you have mine. We need to be careful." Her scent seemed so familiar to him, as if he'd known it all his life.

Katie felt as if her skin was electric. Alan's touch brought such pleasure! She wasn't sure if she could hold out much longer...that's how badly she wanted him. With a huge boost of willpower, she pushed him away.

"Let's...let's sit down, Alan, before we totally lose control," said Katie breathlessly. "Otherwise, we'll lose control right here on the front porch!"

Alan laughed mildly. "I know! I almost backed you over to the porch swing!"

They sat in the rocking chairs again.

"Okay, we need to talk about something else...take our minds off of...well, just off," said Alan.

Katie took a deep breath and nodded. "You're right." She tried to focus her thoughts. "Let's go trade the car in tomorrow and get a pickup. We need it for the seed."

Alan nodded. "Sure, Katie. You're right, we do need it. Let's go right after Carol Grace goes to school."

Katie nodded. "And we can pick up some seed after we're done trading for the truck. Mackie's can deliver the rest."

They rocked a little more.

Hesitantly, Katie asked, "Do you want to move into the main house?"

Alan said, "I'd love to, but not yet. I don't want Carol Grace to get the wrong idea."

Katie nodded again.

"I've never felt this way this quickly about anyone, Katie," continued Alan. "I look back at the years I've wasted since we were in high school, and I kick myself for not letting my feelings be known back then."

Katie pondered that for a moment. "I'm not sure that it would have worked then, Alan. I mean, I was very much in love with Mark. Nothing can change that. But, for the first time since his death, I'm ready to love again...I'm already in love again." She glanced at him. "I'm in love with you. It feels right...like it should be, and always will be."

"And I'm in love with you, Katie. And not just you. I love Carol Grace as if she were my own. I'm ready to give up being a cop, and turn myself into a husband, a father, and a farmer, all in one big move." He smiled. "It's amazing what a man will do for the woman he loves. But..."

"You have to wind up the Turley case first," finished Katie.

Alan nodded. "And it's possible they'll come to Sardis County. Winstead, my partner, knew an awful lot about me. He could have told them everything he knew, if he was in enough pain." He shrugged, and looked off into the distance. "I'm the last witness. If the Giambinis kill me, chances are slim that Turley will be convicted. Turley's going to be desperate, because he knows that Mickey Giambini will kill him if it goes to trial, and he may be likely to kill Turley, even if Turley kills me. Turley has brought too much attention to the Giambinis, especially after Justice Security bought the building across the street from the Giambinis' building and installed the FBI's surveillance team rent-free."

Katie laughed derisively. "Justice Security. Carol Grace and I were in the city park the day that the German mercenaries tried to kill them." She shook her head. "It was one of the reasons that I decided to move back here from the city. I didn't feel very secure that day."

"I was there for the mop-up. The FBI says that it isn't Justice Security's fault. This Esteban Fernandez has sworn to kill them all, and he put a multi-million dollar bounty on their heads," replied Alan. "It's bringing killers out of the woodwork trying to collect the blood money. They're just defending themselves."

"Don't misunderstand me, Alan," said Katie, matter-of-factly. "I understand all of that, but I don't want a stray bullet from *their* war hurting or killing *my* daughter. She's far safer here."

They rocked in silence for a few moments. Both of them realized that they had distracted themselves enough, and that the threat of losing control and throwing themselves at each other had passed.

"I agree with you there, Katie," said Alan. He stood. "And, with that, I'm going to check on the chickens and go to bed. Alone, darn it."

Katie stood. "I think I'll go upstairs, too. And wish you were beside me."

The couple held each other for a long time, because their goodnight kiss seemed to never end.

FRIDAY MORNING, AFTER breakfast, Carol Grace left for school. She had to run because breakfast had been a little late. The teen had grabbed a final piece of toast and ate it as she ran down the driveway to catch the bus. Little Bit watched her walk down the driveway through the screen door, until the school bus picked up Carol Grace. Little Bit snorted, barked once, then ran up the stairs and parked herself on Carol Grace's bed. She would stay there until the teen returned home that afternoon.

There hadn't been a lot of conversation at breakfast. Carol Grace was too excited for small talk, for two reasons: The first one was that the in-school suspension for her and Mary ended today, and Mary was coming to spend the night tonight...and maybe the whole weekend, if she could talk both moms into it.

Katie and Alan had kissed each other good morning as they shared breakfast duties. Of course, it had been a long kiss. And a long embrace. And another long kiss...and another...until...

"Oh, my *God*, will you two stop already? Is that all you think about?" said Carol Grace. She had just entered the kitchen and flopped down into her chair at the table. "You guys are going to *ruin* my breakfast!"

The adults smiled at each other, and each one kissed Carol Grace on the head. She tried to duck, but to no avail.

"*Stop* it! You'll mess up my hair!" cried Carol Grace.

"You'll live, sweetheart," Alan told her.

Katie inspected Carol Grace's head. "Not a hair out of place."

Carol Grace rolled her eyes, and started thinking about the day.

After Carol Grace ran out the kitchen door for the bus, Katie and Alan put the breakfast dishes into the kitchen sink. They went outside and pulled the car around to the parking area in front of the house. Katie began taking out the personal items that seem to find themselves to most cars, and Alan began vacuuming the carpets and upholstery. They planned to run the car through the automatic carwash in Perry, and take it over to the car dealership.

The couple focused on the job at hand...and stopped occasionally, for a kiss, for a hug, for a simple touch of their hands. They weren't really aware of much of their surroundings. Alan, the trained cop, had relaxed his observation skills. After all, this was Sardis County, miles away from the city. *Really, there isn't much chance of being found here.*

Alan was wrong.

If Alan had been more observant, he might have noticed the occasional glint of morning sunshine reflecting on something all the way at the end of the driveway and in the woods across the road.

MOSES TURLEY LOWERED the binoculars.

"*Found* you, you son of a bitch!" said Turley, mostly to himself.

Tolani opened his mouth to ask who his boss had found, but Gino Blasi put his hand over Tolani's mouth before a sound was made. Tolani, wisely, nodded his understanding and kept quiet.

Joe Flore eased quietly up to Turley's side. "Should we go take him out now, Moses?"

Turley raised his binoculars. "No, not yet. There's some broad with him. We got a little time. We'll wait and see if we can catch him alone."

As Turley watched, he saw Alan and Katie get into the car and start toward the road.

"Here they come! Everybody out of sight!" hissed Turley.

The men ducked, hiding themselves behind bushes and trees. The car came to the end of the driveway, stopped, then turned toward town.

Turley, who had quickly ducked under some bushes, did not move as the car fell out of sight.

Tolani said, "Hey, boss, you can get up now. They're gone."

"Be glad to," replied Turley, quietly. "Just as soon as one of you comes and kills this fucking snake."

ALAN DROVE SLOWLY AS they turned toward town. He was looking across the road at a car that could barely be seen through the trees.

"What is it, Alan?" asked Katie.

"There's a car parked in the trees."

Katie smiled. "It's just some hunter, or someone looking for ginseng. A lot of ginseng grows around here."

"You're probably right," he said, as he sped up.

BLASI EASED OVER TO Turley's right. As he did, the snake, a rattler, began shaking its tail, making its signature sound. Its head was drawn back into its striking position, and it was looking directly at Turley.

Blasi pulled his gun, took careful aim at the snake, and blew its head to pieces. Bits of snake blood and meat splattered Turley, as he jumped up and away from the spot in which he had been kneeling.

Turley's breathing was fast and deep. He had almost wet himself when the gun fired because he had been so frozen with fright. He was trembling slightly.

Finally, Turley said, "Thanks, Gino."

Blasi shrugged. "No problem, boss."

Tolani, with a smile on his face, said, "Fuckin' snake almost gotcha, didn't it, boss?"

Turley punched Tolani in the eye. To Blasi and Flore, he said, "Pick him up, and let's go check out that farm."

CAROL GRACE AND MARY were suffering through their final day of in-school suspension. Mrs. Buckner had finally eased up on the girls, and talked with them a bit during the morning. They confided in the teacher that they had become best friends, and that Mary would be spending the night at Junior's Farm.

"That's wonderful news, girls!" said Buckner. "I'm sure it will make Principal Wallace happy, too!"

Both girls had stayed away from wishing. The incident in the lunchroom with the cheerleader had made the girls realize that they had to be careful, and it had also provided an interesting side effect: word of the incident had circulated, and none of the students picked on either Mary or Carol Grace.

None of the students had anything at all to do with either of them.

It bothered Mary that no one had anything to do with her, even the girls that used to be her friends. She felt very small and very insignificant. Then she thought of Carol Grace, the new friend that she had made, and her spirits lifted. They just clicked, and that made up for a lot of the grief that she felt.

Carol Grace, on the other hand, was very content to be friends with Mary. In the city, Carol Grace counted herself lucky to have one or two friends in school that weren't into drugs, gangs, or shoplifting. In the city, she always had to be on her guard with girls her age, and most of them seemed to be headed for a poor life in Hooker Hollow. In Sardis County, she could relax with Mary's friendship, confident that they would watch out for each other.

At lunch, the girls sat alone at their table. They talked about what they would do over the weekend. Teresa, the unfortunate cheerleader that had been the object of the girls' wishing wrath, sat quietly with her friends, and kept sneaking glances at Carol Grace and Mary. While her body had returned to normal, it would take a while for her hair to grow back. Although it was growing back at a more rapid pace than normal, Teresa wore a scarf to hide the fact that her hair wasn't what it was.

Finally, Teresa rose from her table and walked hesitantly to the table that Carol Grace and Mary were sharing.

"H-hi," said Teresa timidly.

Carol Grace shared a look with Mary, and then replied, "Hi, Teresa."

Teresa clenched her hands together to keep them still. She stared at the floor. "I, uh...I just wanted to say I'm sorry about what I said."

Carol Grace looked at Mary, asking a silent question. Mary, wide-eyed, nodded slightly.

"All forgotten," said Carol Grace. "Want to sit with us?"

Teresa looked at the other two. A smile played around her face, and her attitude brightened suddenly. "I'd *love* it!" She pulled out a chair, and joined in the conversation.

Soon, two more girls from Teresa's table came over to sit with them. Then, girls from all over the cafeteria had joined Carol Grace and Mary.

They were accepted, and popular. Just like *that!* And no wishing had been involved.

Carol Grace and Mary tapped knuckles, smiling at each other. It was going to be all right after all!

KATIE DROVE THE NEW truck off of the car lot. It was last year's model, and she had gotten it for a good price, with a generous trade-in amount for the sedan. The truck had a crew cab, with a full-size bed, four wheel drive, and was built for towing trailers. It was shiny and red. Alan had liked it, and pronounced it fit to be a good farm truck.

Katie liked it, too. Driving it, however, was going to take some getting used to.

"It's like driving a tank!" exclaimed Katie, as she tried to negotiate the turn into traffic.

Alan laughed. "At least you're learning how to handle it here, and not in the city!"

"Oh, my God!" said Katie, laughing. "There's no *way!* Could you imagine trying to squeeze down Hooker Hollow with this thing?"

"You could do it. You'll be surprised how quickly you get used to it."

"If you say so. Okay, next stop is the Co-Op. We're ordering seed, buying more chicken feed, and looking for a horse trailer."

"Are we still planning on running some cattle, Katie?"

"I'd like to."

"Have you considered a small dairy operation? We could convert the barn easily."

Katie considered this for a moment. "Let's see how things go with regular cattle first, okay? I'm afraid that dairy farming might take more time than we have."

Alan nodded. "Whatever you want, Katie, is what I want."

Katie smiled as she turned into the Co-Op.

TURLEY AND HIS MEN parked in a far corner of the turnaround in front of Katie's farmhouse. The four men got out of the car.

"How do you want to do this, Moses?" asked Blasi.

Turley scanned the farmhouse, the outbuildings, and the barn. To the three men, he said, "Just a minute. I want to get a feel for the place, and then I'll call Rizzo. Let him know what's going on. Everybody spread out and give me a little privacy."

Blasi, Flore, and Tolani moved away from Turley, giving him plenty of room. Tolani still rubbed his eye, worried that it would turn black from Turley's punch.

Turley scanned the area again, counting on his subconscious to pick up anything that his eyes missed. He felt that the place was empty for the moment. He took out his cell phone and called Rizzo.

"Rizzo."

"It's Turley."

"Mose! What's cookin'?"

"Not much, Rizzo. Listen, we may have found where Blake is hiding."

"Hey, that's great. Where's that? Where are you guys? You still in Sardis County?"

Moses Turley wasn't stupid. Rizzo's questions sounded innocent enough, but something in Rizzo's tone triggered an alarm in Turley's mind. It was the feeling he got when a mark had a better hand than he held. Like he was about to lose everything.

Turley felt strongly that the only reason Rizzo wanted to know where they were was because Mickey Giambini had ordered Rizzo to take care of the four of them. He glanced at the three men that worked for him. Turley decided that none of them needed to die, not even Tolani.

All of this went through his mind in less than a second.

"We're on I-55 right now, following Blake down to New Orleans. We stumbled onto him by accident in Sardis County, and started following him.

Flore overheard him tell a guy in a gas station that he was heading to Bourbon Street."

"Sounds good, Mose. Gimme a call when you get there, would ya? Let me know where you're staying. I might see if the boss'll gimme a couple of days off. I ain't been to the French Quarter in forever, you know?"

"I hear you, Rizzo, but just barely. We must be coming to a spot with bad service. I'll call you when we know where we're staying."

"Okay, Mose. Get this guy, willya?"

"It's taken care of."

Turley disconnected the call. He looked at the phone angrily. *Rizzo, you cocksucker! You're not taking me out!*

"C'mere, guys! Got something else to worry about!" called Turley.

When the men gathered around him, Turley explained what had just happened, and what he thought was going on.

"Why does Mickey wanna kill us, Mose?" asked Flore.

"Because we got arrested. We haven't killed this cop. We brought too much attention down on the Giambini family. Mickey probably told Rizzo to take us out even if we get this cop."

"But, boss," said Tolani. "If we kill this cop, don't that get rid of the attention?"

Turley shook his head. "Think about it, Tolani! If we wipe out this cop, who gets the blame? The Giambini family! And if they're getting more attention, it makes it harder for the family to do business. So Mickey wipes us out for bringing down more attention. On the other hand, if we *don't* get the cop, Mickey wipes us out so that there's no trial. Or, the cop kills us somehow. It's win-win-win all the way around for the Giambinis if we're out of the picture!"

"So, you're sayin' we're fucked no matter what," said Blasi.

Flore nodded. "Yeah, Gino, we're fucked."

"Well, I don't know about *you* guys, but I got money squirreled away, and I got a passport with a name that isn't mine. I'm gonna kill this cop, and then I'm goin' to South America somewhere!"

The three men all looked at each other.

Finally, Blasi spoke. "We all got them things, too, boss. Mind if we tag along?"

Turley smiled. *Bless their non-trusting hearts. Something you learn the hard way in this business. We could set ourselves up real pretty down there...bribe a few locals, set up a few good games, make a few bucks. Mickey won't bother coming after us there.*

"When we gonna kill the cop, Moses?" asked Tolani.

Turley noticed that Tolani didn't use the word 'boss' this time. That meant that the boys thought of him as an equal now. And that was fine and dandy with him.

"Let's do it tomorrow night. We'll take him out, and have a little fun with the broad. Then, we take *her* out, too."

There were murmurs of agreement, and a chuckle or two.

"Okay, let's check out the house. We need a way to sneak up on them."

"OKAY, MIZ MONTGOMERY," said the man at the Co-Op. "We got your feed loaded into your truck. We'll deliver the seed sometime Monday morning, if that's okay."

Katie nodded. "That's great, Lester. Thank you!"

Lester smiled. "Thank *you*, Katie. It's good to see that Junior's Farm is coming back to life!"

As Katie and Alan left the Co-Op, several people greeted them. Well, greeted Katie. Not everyone remembered Alan yet, and that was probably a good thing.

Outside, Alan said, "I never realized all those years ago how popular your grandparents were."

"It *is* pretty awesome, isn't it?"

"Yes, it is! Okay, where to now?"

"Mackie's. I have to get food for the cookout."

"Wouldn't it be cheaper if we went to that big box store?"

Katie snorted. "Sure, it would be cheaper. But, they're not our neighbors, are they? I'd rather pay a few cents more per item and support local people than pay some conglomerate. That's what's wrong with our economy now!"

"You're right, of course. Hey, would you mind dropping me off at Billy's office until you're done? I should probably call Lieutenant Pyne."

"Sure. Not a word to Billy about Phoebe!"

"My lips are sealed."

Katie smiled and replied, "Your lips are yummy!"

To prove it, Alan leaned over and kissed Katie. Several times.

"HEY, TOLANI, C'MERE," said Turley.

Turley was standing beside the twin doors that opened into the cellar. They were secured by a single large padlock.

Tolani wandered over. "What's up?"

Turley pointed to the padlock. "Can you pick that?"

Tolani gave a "you gotta be kidding" look, and said, "Mose. If it has a lock, I can open it."

"Then show me."

Tolani chuckled, and pulled out a small leather case. He opened it and selected a couple of lock-picking tools. The lock was lying on the ground thirty seconds later.

Turley slapped Tolani on the back. "Great job, Tolani! Gino, why don't you stay up here and keep watch? The rest of us will check out the cellar."

Blasi nodded.

As Turley, Flore, and Tolani turned toward the cellar stairs, Tolani said, smiling, "Hey, Mose! Think there's any more snakes down there?"

Turley stopped in his tracks. He turned slowly to Tolani. Tolani quickly dropped his smile.

Very quietly, Turley said, "I don't know, Tolani. Why don't you go first and find out?" He pointed to the stairs.

Tolani looked from Turley's face, to his pointing finger, finally to the dark cellar. He looked again at Turley's darkened, angry face. He gulped, turned, and slowly led the way down the stairs.

ALAN STOOD AT THE DRIVER'S side door of the new truck. He was kissing Katie goodbye.

"I shouldn't be more than an hour, Alan. If you get ready to leave, walk over to Mackie's and find me, okay?" said Katie.

"Yes, dear," Alan said meekly.

Katie gave him a look. With just a hint of sarcasm, she said, "The correct phrase is 'Yes, your worship.'" She then threw her nose into the air.

Alan laughed and said, "Yes, your worship!" As Katie started to pull away from the Sheriff's office, he called, "Be careful!"

Katie honked the horn in return as she drove to Mackie's.

Alan watched until she turned toward the store, then walked into the Sheriff's office. To the deputy behind the glass partition, Alan said, "Is Billy in?"

The deputy nodded, and buzzed Alan in.

Billy was sitting at his desk, frowning at some paperwork on his desk. He looked up at Alan and said, "I got a moron that I want you to meet."

Alan raised his eyebrows questioningly. "Okay."

"Sit down, Alan. Before the moron gets here, I'd like to ask you something," said Billy.

Alan sat in one of the two chairs in front of Sheriff Napier's desk. "Sure. Shoot."

"Are you happy working in the city?"

Alan started to answer, then held back and thought for a few seconds. "I used to be. I'm not now. I mean, look at me! I'm hiding out in Sardis County so that some mobsters don't kill me! What kind of life is that? So, to answer your question, no. I'm not happy working in the city."

Billy clasped his hands on top of his big desk calendar. "Wanna come work for me?"

Alan's mouth hung open. He couldn't speak.

Billy held his hands out. "Now, wait...it doesn't have to be full-time, although I could use you. If it's only part-time, I can use you. I know you and Katie seem to have hit it off, and I don't want it messed up by you feeling that you haven't got choices." Billy took a deep breath. "Tell the truth, I wish I could get the Perry City Council to name you city Police Chief, but I can't convince them that Godfrey Malcolm is *not* the man for the job."

"I thought you were in charge of all law enforcement personnel in Sardis County."

Billy nodded. "I am...with the exception of the Police Chief in the city of Perry. The council kept that power to themselves." He shook his head. "I can order the stinkin' drunk around, but I can't fire him. It *really* gets to me sometimes." He took another deep breath. "That's the moron I want you to meet. He's stopping by for some kind of 'pow-wow', as he puts it. A few months ago, some kind of animal killed a couple of his officers. He claimed that it was an escaped zoo animal, and that it was recaptured. I never saw it, and there's no zoo closer than the city. Lying bastard. But he did have two dead officers...and they all agree on Malcolm's story." He shook his head, then looked at Alan. "So, how about it? Want to come work for me?"

"Mind if I talk it over with Katie first?"

"I'd expect you to. Especially if you're thinking about marrying her."

Alan found himself about to make a smart-aleck reply, and stopped himself. "You know, I just might ask her. Billy, I'm flat-out, totally in love with that woman! I can't think about anything *but* her. And Carol Grace would make a wonderful stepdaughter. Hell, I might even see about adopting her, if she can stand me as her father."

Billy smiled. "I'm glad for both of you, Alan. If the farm works out, and you come to work for me, everybody will be happy!"

Someone knocked on Billy's office door as it opened. A tall man with a barrel-shaped upper body atop thin, skinny legs walked in without waiting for an answer. The man was dressed in a uniform, and had an embroidered patch on his uniform shirt that read, "Chief". Alan assumed, correctly, this was Godfrey Malcolm.

Malcolm began talking as soon as he came through the door. "Look, Billy, I don't want my officers patrolling the damn county in city cars! I only have so much money in my budget, and I'll be damned if I spend it on gas for..." He stopped as he finally noticed Alan sitting quietly. "Oh, sorry, I didn't know anyone was here."

Alan could actually smell the alcohol on Malcolm's breath. He waved his hand in front of his face and wrinkled his nose.

Billy noticed this, and said quietly, "Godfrey. Have you been drinking?"

Malcolm stood to his full height. "Napier, that's a damn lie!"

Billy, holding his temper in check, said, "No, Godfrey, that's a question. A damn lie will be if you answer 'no.'"

Malcolm, red, rheumy eyes focusing, said, "Maybe I had a couple of beers with my lunch."

"A couple?" Billy shook his head, then raised his eyes to Malcolm's. "Did you drive here, Godfrey?"

"Why?"

"Because I may not be able to fire you, but I sure as hell can arrest you for driving under the influence. The city council would certainly take notice of that, don't you think?"

Malcolm let that sink in through the haze of alcohol that was fogging his brain a bit. He answered slowly. "I had an officer drive me over."

"Is he still here?"

"No, I told him to walk back to the station."

"So, I'm assuming that you'll be walking back, too?"

It was obvious that the question had caught Malcolm flatfooted. His surprise slowly registered, then turned to disgust. "Yeah, I guess I am."

Alan had to turn away to hide his smile.

Billy said, "Good. I'll have one of my men drop your cruiser at the police station. Did you leave the keys in it?"

"Yeah, they're still...," Malcolm stopped talking as he realized what he said.

"Great! Well, thanks for stopping by, Godfrey! Enjoy your walk!"

Malcolm, confused, mumbled something like, "See you later," and left the office.

Alan burst out laughing. "*That's* the Perry Police Chief?"

Billy, smiled and nodded. "Oh, yeah, that's him. I can't figure out what he's got on the city council, but it must be something big to keep his job." He laughed derisively. "If we had a high crime rate, I'd be pushing harder...*much* harder to get rid of him, but we just don't have much crime at all in Sardis County."

"Well, your last statement just convinced me, Billy," said Alan. "I'll take the job as full-time deputy, with the option to go part-time if the farm needs me."

"Great! I can sure use the help, Alan!"

The men shook hands.

"Well, I guess I'd better call Lieutenant Pyne and give him the news. He's not going to like it."

"Don't tell him where you're going, Alan...not until you testify."

"I know...not knowing who hired me away will make him *really* hit the roof!"

AFTER THREE TRIES, Katie got the truck eased into the parking space at Mackie's. She laughed at herself, and laughed at her sudden flash of what would happen if she had tried parallel parking the truck back in the city.

She went inside the store. Phoebe was in her usual checkout lane, and she looked up as Katie came in. A huge smile broke out over her face, and she waved at Katie.

Katie, smiling, waved back, and started shopping.

When Katie finished, she got into Phoebe's line.

"Now, Phoebe, if you need to talk to Mary, you call anytime. The girls are going to have so much fun, and I bet that they spend most of their time playing with the chickens!" said Katie.

Phoebe laughed. "You're probably right. My oldest has a cat, and I think Mary loves that cat more than Pamela loves him!"

"Our appointments are at nine in the morning. Do you want me to pick you up, or do you want to come to the farm first?" asked Katie.

"Do you mind picking me up?" asked Phoebe. "If it's going to take us all day, I'll just ride with you, if you can bring Mary and I home tomorrow night."

"Sure, Phoebe! Sounds like a plan!" said Katie, as she paid for her purchases. "Okay, I'll see you in the morning"

"Bye, Katie! I can't wait!"

"I'M SORRY, LIEUTENANT, but that's how it is. You have my notice, and I'll be starting work at this other job in two weeks," said Alan. He was talking with Lieutenant Pyne. Pyne was not taking the news very well.

"Look, Alan, you're the best undercover man I've got. Is it money? I can hit the captain up for a raise for you, but I can't promise anything...," said Pyne. "You need vacation? I can probably swing that, too...and with pay!"

"I'm sorry, Lieutenant. I have to do this."

"Okay, Alan, I understand. But, you better believe I want some information when this trial is over!"

Alan smiled. "You bet, Stan. I'll fill you in on all of it as soon as I can."

"You take care, now, Alan, you hear?"

"Yes, sir. You, too." Alan disconnected the call.

He turned and went back inside the sheriff's office, and knocked on Billy's door.

"Come in!" called Billy.

Alan opened the door and stuck his head inside. "Two weeks from today, Billy. I'll officially be your deputy."

Billy smiled, stood, and walked around his desk, holding out his hand. He took Alan's hand in his and pumped it furiously.

"Man, that is such a relief!" said Billy. "You don't realize how much I really need you here!"

"Well, good, Billy. Now all we have to do is tell Katie."

Billy looked pensive. "I think I'll let you do that, Alan," he said in a serious tone. "Right after you ask her to marry you."

Alan laughed. "Hey, she should be here any time. Want to see the new truck?"

"Oh, yeah!"

"LOOKS LIKE A REGULAR cellar, Mose," said Flore.

Turley nodded. "Yeah." He pointed. "There's the stairs."

"That's great, boss, but what if the door up there is locked tomorrow night?" asked Blasi.

"Not a problem. We still got our savant," said Turley, throwing a thumb toward Tolani.

"Yeah, locks ain't nuthin' to me, Gino," said Tolani, as he backed up with his arms spread out. He was smiling as he spoke, until he backed against a small tool box left on the floor, tripped, and fell backwards. He landed hard on his back, but managed to keep his head from hitting the ground. He said, "Ooof!" when he landed. His momentum caused him to skid backwards a few inches, until his head was under the shelves on the wall. Then he laid still, trembling with laughter at his own clumsiness.

Turley and the other began laughing. They laughed loud and long, especially at Tolani's surprised look as he fell over backwards.

Finally, Tolani said, "Hey, Moses, come look at this!"

Turley walked over and squatted down beside Tolani. "What?"

Tolani pointed. "There's a button here." He pressed it.

The hidden wall in the cellar slid open.

The four men stared at it, wide-eyed.

"Holy shit, boss, did you know that was there?" asked Flore.

Turley shook his head slowly. "No, no idea."

Blasi pointed to a spot just inside the tunnel. "There's the button to open the door from that side, and there's a light switch."

Turley took a deep breath and said, "Let's go check it out. You go first, Tolani."

"THAT'S THE DEAL, KATIE," said Alan. "What do you think?"

Katie and Alan were sitting on the truck's tailgate, outside the sheriff's office. Alan had just told her about Billy's job offer.

Katie looked at her hands, then glanced at Alan. "Why are you asking me, Alan?"

Alan squirmed. "Well, I just...you know, I wanted...well..."

Katie, with a small smile, said, "Why, Alan, are you tongue-tied?"

Alan nodded.

"Well, I guess if you can't spit the words out, you have nothing to say. Am I right?"

Alan shook his head.

"Then, don't you think you should say what's on your mind?"

"Katie, will you marry me?" blurted Alan.

Katie's mouth opened and closed twice before she could form words.

"Yes," she said simply.

Alan nodded. "Good. That's good."

The couple finally met each other's eyes.

"Oh, my God," said Katie. "Alan, I love you."

Alan smiled. "I love you, too, Katie."

They held each other for a long time. Neither of them saw Billy peeking out the window at them, and neither of them saw him smile.

THE STRAW-COVERED WOODEN hatch popped open, and Tolani's head popped up. They were at the last stop in the tunnels, the equipment shed at the back of the main compound. A good-sized patch of woods stretched behind the shed.

Tolani climbed out, followed by Blasi, then Flore, and, finally, Turley.

The men looked around at their surroundings.

Turley started nodding.

"That's it, then," he said. "Tomorrow, before dark, we sneak down here through the fields, get into the tunnel, and sneak up on Blake and his girl after dark. We'll take care of them, then we're Brazil-bound, boys!"

Turley started back down the ladder. "Let's go, before we get caught. We'll stash some guns in the tunnel. That'll be our insurance."

One by one, they climbed back down the ladder, made their way through the tunnel to the cellar, and left Junior's Farm the way they had come.

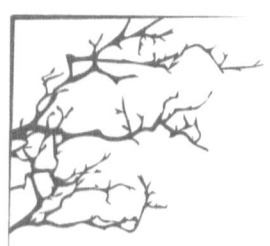

Chapter 12

Alan and Katie made one more stop before they went home. They stopped at Perry Jewelers, at Alan's insistence.

"We're engaged, and I'm going to make sure that you have an engagement ring," he said to Katie.

Katie tried to protest, but Alan would hear none of it. And he told Katie to pick out the one she wanted, and to hell with the cost.

"Katie, this is the only one I've ever wanted to buy, and it's the only one I ever *will* buy. So, it's going to be something that you'll be proud to wear," he told her.

Katie, flustered, was unable to change Alan's mind. They stopped at Perry Jewelers.

Katie found a ring that she liked. It was a simple gold ring, with six prongs holding a quarter-carat diamond. It fit perfectly.

Alan paid with his credit card.

Katie questioned this. "Aren't you afraid that the Giambinis will hear about that purchase somehow?"

Alan shook his head. "The chances of that are slim, Katie."

Once they were back inside the truck, Alan slipped the ring onto the third finger of her left hand. "I love you, Katie. I promise that I'll be a good husband for you, and a good role model for Carol Grace. And I will love you until my last breath."

Katie had tears in her eyes. "And I will love you, Alan, until the day I die."

They kissed then, for quite a long while. After that, they headed home.

CAROL GRACE AND MARY got off of the bus and told Mary McKinnon to have a good weekend. They raced each other down the driveway until they reached the front porch. Both girls were giggling and breathing heavily.

The front door was locked.

"Mom must be gone somewhere," said Carol Grace. "She'll be back soon, I'm sure. Come on around to the kitchen door, Mary. I've got a key."

The girls ran around to the side of the house, and went inside through the kitchen. Carol Grace led the way to her room, and opened the door.

Little Bit started jumping and barking excitedly around both girls. Mary finally caught the puppy and gave it a hug. Little Bit returned the affection by licking Mary's face repeatedly.

Finally, Mary put Little Bit onto the floor and looked around.

"Wow, Carol Grace! This room is *huge!*" said Mary. "And you have it all to yourself!" She ran her hand along the end of the canopy bed. "I have to share a room with my sisters, Pam and Catherine. My little brother, Derek, has his own room."

"So you don't mind sharing the bed with me tonight?" asked Carol Grace. "We have a guest room, if you'd like to use it instead."

Mary gave Carol Grace a look. "Are you *kidding?* We're going to stay up all night, and I'll fill you in on some of the boys at school."

Carol Grace replied, "Yeah, and we can put nail polish on our fingers and toes!"

The girls heard the sound of a vehicle coming up the driveway.

"Must be Mom," said Carol Grace. "Come on, you gotta meet Alan!"

They ran down the stairs and outside. In the turnaround, a big crew cab pickup truck was parked.

"Um, Carol Grace," said Mary. "Is that your mom's truck?"

The driver's door opened, and Katie climbed out. "Hi, Mary! Welcome to Junior's Farm! What do you girls think of the new truck?"

A delighted look was pasted on Carol Grace's face. "Oh, Mom, I *love* it!" she gushed. Both girls ran to the truck to look it over.

Alan had come around to the driver's side of the truck. "Now, listen, this is a farm truck. We can't have it covered with girls' fingerprints." Then he winked at Carol Grace.

Carol Grace grinned back, and started putting her hands all over the truck. "Oh, too late! Looks like we've done it now!"

Mary smiled shyly.

Katie noticed. "Carol Grace, aren't you going to introduce Mary to Alan?"

"Oh, yeah! Mary, this is Alan Blake. He's our farm hand. He's helping us out for a while."

Alan shook Mary's hand and said, "Nice to meet you, Miss Smalls."

"Nice to meet you, too," said Mary, with a blush. "Mom says you were on the football team with Sheriff Billy."

"Phoebe is right. We all graduated from Perry High School together," said Alan.

"Mom says you like Katie," said Mary.

Alan nodded. "Your mom is right again, except that I don't just like Katie. I love Katie. And I love Carol Grace, even *if* she's a grimy old teenager!"

"I'm not *grimy*," said Carol Grace, hitting Alan on the arm. Then she smiled. "I'm just a little dusty is all."

Everyone laughed at Carol Grace's joke.

"Carol Grace, I have a serious question to ask you," said Alan.

"Okay," replied Carol Grace.

"What would you say if I told you that I've asked your mom to marry me?"

Mary's eyes became so wide that they quickly dominated her facial features.

Carol Grace quickly cut her eyes to her mother. Katie was holding her left hand up to her face, with the ring facing out toward the girls. The teenager's face became ecstatic, and she squealed with delight. She took her mother's hand in hers, and was looking at the ring. She gushed over it, as did Mary and Katie. They stood together, holding hands and giggling.

Alan cleared his throat. The women turned toward him.

"You haven't answered my question, Carol Grace," Alan said, with a serious look on his face. "Before you answer, I'm asking you about this because it involves you and I just as much as it involves your mother and I. I love your mother. I love you. I want to be your stepdad, and, if we both feel strongly about it, someday I would love to adopt you as my own daughter. But, right now, because this involves you, too, I'm asking if you'd like me to marry your mother."

Carol Grace was amazed. Alan was talking to her as if her opinion mattered to him. *But, then, I guess it does matter to him. He wouldn't be asking me otherwise.*

"Alan," the teen said, "if you will love my mom always, and love me, and be good to us, and help us with the farm...then, yes, I'd be happy to be part of a family with you." She went to Alan and hugged him fiercely.

Alan, surprised, hugged the girl back tightly, and kissed the top of her head.

"Thank you, honey," he said.

With tears in her eyes, Carol Grace said, "You're welcome." Then she hugged her mother.

Katie said, "Why don't you and Mary help us carry these groceries inside? Then you can show Mary your chickens, and we'll have dinner in an hour or so."

LATE THAT NIGHT, THE girls were in Carol Grace's room, playing loud music, talking, and giggling.

Downstairs, Katie and Alan were snuggled on the love seat, with the television on. They weren't watching it, but it was playing, throwing a warm light around the living room.

Talking quietly while the laugh tracks and corny dramatic music played in the background, the couple held hands, and took frequent kissing breaks.

Finally, Katie asked, "When do you think we should have the wedding?"

"I don't see any need to wait, do you?" replied Alan.

Smiling, Katie shook her head. "No."

"What kind of wedding do you want?"

"Something small. I don't want anything fancy." She ran her finger over his cheek. "We aren't fancy people, are we?"

Alan shook his head. "No. Well, we could have Billy track down a Justice Of The Peace tomorrow, I guess."

"Can't tomorrow. I have a date with a friend and a salon."

"Oh, yeah." Alan smiled. "Maybe they'll hit it off, and Billy and Feeble will be a couple again."

"I wish you wouldn't call her 'Feeble'," said Katie.

"It's just a habit, honey, I'm sorry."

"I think if we all support her, she'll stay sober. And happy."

"I think so, too."

"Do you think Billy will give her another chance?"

Alan smiled. "If he can swallow his pride, yes."

Katie was silent for a while. "Alan, do you think that the Giambinis will ever track you down here?

"No. How could they? Even if James talked before he died, we would have heard about strangers asking after me by now."

"I guess you're right."

CRAAACKK!

The sound of a tree falling outside came to them.

Katie jumped, and her eyes widened. "Oh, *no!* I forgot the protection spell!"

They went out onto the front porch. Katie quickly closed her eyes, concentrated, and murmured the words to the spell. Once again, the blue light surged from within her and traveled down her arm, spilling out from her outstretched hand.

The dome quietly settled over the farm once more. As it settled, a howl came from the woods across the road.

It wasn't a howl that either of them had ever heard.

"What the *hell* was that?" asked Alan.

"I don't know, and I don't want to know," replied Katie. "I guess I'd better tell you what else Aunt Margo told me." She then told Alan about the open doorway to Hell.

"So, that could have been something from Hell?" asked Alan.

"Maybe. Or maybe it was a coyote with a funny howl."

They looked out across the fields, and Alan gulped.

Finally, Katie said, "Alan, go to the bunkhouse and get your things. I'd feel better if you slept in the house now." She shyly met his eyes. "In my room. I mean, *our* room." Then she smiled.

"I think it's time," said Alan, and walked to the bunkhouse to retrieve his belongings.

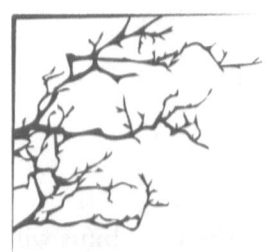

Chapter 13

Saturday morning, bright and early, Katie awakened. She was snuggled against Alan, and his arm was around her.

She smiled.

It had been years since she had felt such happiness, and Katie took a few moments to revel in it.

Then, knowing that she had to hurry to pick up Phoebe and make their salon appointments, Katie rose naked from under the covers. She leaned over and kissed Alan's lips without waking him.

Katie quickly hopped into the shower, then dressed. She applied a minimum amount of makeup, because she knew that the salon would do a fantastic job making her over.

She again kissed Alan's sleeping form, and left the bedroom.

Katie stopped in front of Carol Grace's room, and eased the door open. Both girls were sound asleep, with Little Bit sleeping contentedly on her back between them. Smiling, Katie eased the door closed again and went quietly down the stairs.

She grabbed an apple and a banana for breakfast, got into the truck, and drove over to Phoebe's place.

"GOOD MORNING, GENTLEMEN!" Turley said, with a cheerful tone in his voice. "How did you sleep?"

"I slept like a baby, Mose," said Tolani.

"Yeah – he shit himself and cried all night!" said Blasi.

All four men laughed at the joke.

"Let's go get breakfast, boys," said Turley. "My treat!"

"You're in an awful good mood, Moses," said Flore. "What's up?"

"Look at it," replied Turley. "Tonight we kill off the last witness to anything we've done here, and we're leaving for a new life someplace else. Why wouldn't I be happy?"

PHOEBE CLIMBED INTO Katie's truck. "I'm so excited about today, Katie!"

Katie smiled. "So am I, Phoebe!"

"What's first on the agenda?"

"Well, we're going to that new salon downtown. We're getting our hair done. Then, we're getting manicures, pedicures, and total makeovers. After that, we'll grab some lunch. And, after lunch, we go buy some knockout outfits for tonight that will make the boys' tongues hang out!"

Both women giggled like schoolgirls.

"Oh, Katie, I can't thank you enough for all of this. At least, I'll have a chance at winning Billy again."

"Phoebe, I know this is a touchy subject, and if you think it's none of my business, tell me that – you won't hurt my feelings one bit."

"Okay, sure."

"Do you have any idea who Pam's father might have been?"

Phoebe was quiet, watching the scenery go by. Then, she looked down at her hands. "No. Not one clue. And I don't know who Mary's father is, either. I was drunk both times, and I passed out. And I'm ashamed of it." She lifted her head proudly. "But I know who fathered Derek and Catherine, even if he was a no-good meth-head!"

"Phoebe, there's nothing to be ashamed of. Drunk or not, you were raped! Twice! But both girls are wonderful gifts, even if they came from bad circumstances. Mary's a really special girl, and Carol Grace just loves her!"

Phoebe laughed. "Carol Grace is all that Mary has talked about all week long! I'm so glad they're hitting it off. I guess I can take the girls next weekend, if you're okay with that."

Katie glanced at Phoebe. "Are you sure, Phoebe? I wouldn't want Carol Grace to be any trouble."

"Oh, she won't be, Katie. Four kids or five, it'll be fun!"

"Well, it's okay by me." Katie parked the big pickup. They were at the salon. Katie grabbed Phoebe's hand. "Come on, let's go get pampered!"

The women got out of the truck and went inside.

ALAN WOKE UP. HE HAD been dreaming about kissing Katie, but, when he opened his eyes, Little Bit was licking his face.

"How did you get in here, dog?" asked Alan, as he sat up and rubbed the sleep out of his eyes. Then he realized where he was, and that he was naked. He quickly grabbed his underwear and pants, and put them on.

He could hear the girls giggling outside, and guessed correctly that they were going to the chicken house. *Good. Maybe they won't know that I spent the night in here!* Just as that thought completed itself, Little Bit licked his hand. The thought crossed his mind that Carol Grace may have opened the bedroom door, and let Little Bit into the room. *Uh, oh! I'm caught.*

Well, he would just have to take it like a man.

Alan went downstairs and into the kitchen. The coffee pot was just finishing its brewing cycle. On the table was a plate with three slices of bacon, two biscuits, and two eggs. Beside the plate was a small glass of orange juice and a note. The note was in Carol Grace's handwriting, and it said:

"Dear Alan, I hope you slept well. I think Mom has already gone to town. I cooked breakfast. I hope you like it. Mary and I are going to the chicken house. Back soon! Love, Carol Grace".

Alan looked at the note. He was surprised to feel tears welling in his eyes.

"Love, Carol Grace"

Alan sniffed loudly, wiped his eyes, and tucked the note into his back pocket. No *way* would he ever lose that one!

He sat down and ate a leisurely breakfast, prepared by a child that loved him.

SHERIFF BILLY NAPIER went into The Dragon's Den, the diner on the court square of Perry. He wanted a late breakfast, and he didn't feel like cooking it himself. He sat at the counter on one of the spinning stools, but around the corner so that he could unobtrusively see the entire diner.

Billy decided that he would order a large enough breakfast so that he could skip lunch, and have a big appetite for the cookout at Junior's Farm that night. He ordered four slices of bacon, extra crispy, three hard-fried eggs, and four pieces of buttered toast with jelly. He drank coffee.

As he chatted with Duke Donnell, the owner and chief grill cook, he looked around the diner. In one of the booths, he noticed four men in sport coats eating breakfast. For some reason, his suspicions were aroused by the men, but it was nothing he could put his finger on.

"Duke," said Billy. "Who are those guys?"

Duke glanced over at the four men. "I think Hester told me that they were insurance salesmen or something like that."

Billy nodded. "Have I got a few minutes before my order is ready?"

"Sure."

Billy stood. "Be right back, Duke. I'm just going over to introduce myself." He walked over to the men's booth. "Hello, gentlemen," said Billy. "I'm Billy Napier, the sheriff of Sardis County. You fellas passing through?"

The thin one said, "Yes, we are, Sheriff. We've been here for a couple of days, scouting Perry for a branch office. We're with Avalon Insurance, in the city." He offered his hand, but Billy pretended not to notice. The man put his hand down. "What we've seen so far makes us believe that Perry would make a great town to expand our business."

"Perry's a nice town, and Avalon has good rates," replied Billy. "We'd welcome more options."

"Here, let me give you one of our cards, Sheriff," said the thin man. "Avalon insures business, and government entities as well." He handed Billy a business card, with the well-known Avalon emblem on it. The name on the card was, "Jim Simpson", and had phone numbers listed.

"Thanks!" said Billy, tucking the card into his shirt pocket. "My homeowner's insurance is up soon, and I'll call you for a quote."

The man called Jim said, "Great! We look forward to hearing from you!"

"Hey, Billy!" called Duke. "Your breakfast is ready!"

"You guys have a great visit," said Billy, walking toward his stool at the counter.

"We will, Sheriff! Enjoy your breakfast!" said the man called Jim.

The four men rose, and went to the cash register to settle their bill. They paid, gave Hester a generous tip, and left the diner.

Billy watched, and wondered what had made him so suspicious.

"HOLY SHIT, MOSE! I thought we was dead meat!" said Tolani.

"Yeah, what was on that card, Moses?" asked Blasi.

"The phone numbers for Avalon Insurance, direct to one of the Giambini family's businesses. Any time that phone rings, it gets answered by one of our guys pretending to be Avalon Insurance," answered Turley.

"So, if that nosy sheriff calls...," said Flore.

"...we're covered as employees of Avalon Insurance," finished Turley. "Can't miss. At least, it can't miss until Mickey or Rizzo tells 'em that Jim Simpson doesn't exist anymore. But, we got a couple of days before that happens. By then, we'll be in South America." He looked around the court square. "Let's go back to the motel. We'll lay low until this evening."

"GIRLS, I HAVE TO SAY this: you both look absolutely *beautiful*, if I do say so myself!" said the makeup girl in the salon.

Katie and Phoebe looked at themselves in one of the salon's mirrors. *We do look pretty darn good!* thought Katie to herself. To Phoebe, she said, "You look fantastic, Phoebe! Billy won't know what hit him!"

Phoebe smiled shyly. "You really think so?"

The salon girl interrupted. "Honey, if he doesn't notice you, he doesn't like women!"

The three women giggled and laughed, while Katie paid the salon for the two of them.

As they left, Katie said, "Let's grab a light lunch, and then hit the shops!"

"You're *on!*" replied Phoebe.

THAT AFTERNOON, ALAN was outside with Mary and Carol Grace. They were all throwing a play ball around in some sort of "dodgeball game". Little Bit was running around all three, barking and jumping.

Katie and Phoebe watched the three playing, as the women parked the truck in the turnaround.

"Alan asked me to marry him, Phoebe," said Katie, smiling.

"*Really?*" said Phoebe, with excitement. "You did say 'yes', right?"

Katie nodded. "I did." Katie showed her engagement ring to Phoebe.

"Oooo, nice!" said Phoebe. "What does Carol Grace think about it?"

"She's happy as can be with him," replied Katie.

Both women watched the man playing ball with the two teen girls.

"He's certainly good with them," commented Phoebe.

"I know. It's almost as good as having Mark back."

"Oh, my! Look at Mary! She's having more fun than I've ever seen her have!" Phoebe beamed. "Katie, I'm so glad we're friends. I may never be able to pay you back for today, but you'll always have a friend to count on as long as I'm around."

"Paying me back isn't necessary, Phoebe. You musn't think that way, because if I can put some happiness into your life, it's worth every penny." Katie took the keys out of the ignition. "Come on, let's go tag Alan with that ball!"

The women got out of the truck. Mary saw her mother, and squealed with delight. As she ran to hug Phoebe, Alan threw the soft play ball at the back of Mary's head. It hit the girl, bounced off, and sent Mary off into a batch of giggles.

"I'll get you for that one, Alan!" Mary managed to say between giggles. She hugged her mother tightly. "Oh, Mom, I'm having the best time!"

"That's great, sweetheart!" replied Phoebe.

"Hi, Phoebe," called Alan. He waved, then started making chicken noises at Mary.

Mary squealed, "*Ohhhh!*" She then picked up the ball and threw it at Alan, who dodged the round toy as it flew past him. Carol Grace and Mary both took off after it, with Little Bit running right alongside, while Alan came over to Katie.

He kissed her soundly. "Hi. I missed your face."

Katie looked into his eyes and smiled. "I missed yours, too."

Alan turned to say something to Phoebe, just as the ball hit him on the side of the head. With wide eyes, he turned to the two giggling teens, and snapped his fingers with a circular motion. "Oh, no, you just *di-in't!*"

Both girls moved their heads cockily side-to-side, snapping their fingers in circular motions.

"Uh-*huh!*" said Carol Grace. "*That's* right!"

"Darn *skippy* we did!" said Mary.

Alan started nodding his head and pressing his lips together. He walked over to the truck, and said, "I texted your mothers a little while ago, and asked them to pick something up for me while they were out." He opened the truck door and leaned inside, still talking. He pointed at the ball and said, "Katie, would you hand that to me, please?" Katie did. Alan began rustling in the back seat of the big truck. "See, I knew it was going to turn out this way, so I had to have more ammunition." He came out of the truck with a second play ball in his hand. "Now, I have one for each of you. You *know* what they say about payback!"

"Phoebe, it looks like war! We better duck inside while we can! Come on, I'll give you the tour." They grabbed their bags of purchases, just as Alan pelted each girl with a ball, then started strutting like he was something. The women made it inside the kitchen door just as both girls were driving Alan to the ground with both balls. All three were laughing hard, and the puppy was licking Alan's face.

Inside the house, Katie was talking about the house to Phoebe.

"Please ignore the dishes that Alan and the kids have kindly left for me in the sink," said Katie. "This is the kitchen."

Phoebe was looking around. "Wow! I've never been out here, Katie. This kitchen is gorgeous!"

"It works for us. Come on, let me show you the rest of the house."

"AVALON INSURANCE, THIS is Bert. How may I help you?" said the voice on the other end of the phone.

Billy, sitting behind his sheriff's office desk, said, "Hi. I have a man at the door that says his name is Jim Simpson, and that he's one of your agents. Can you confirm this?"

"I certainly can," said 'Bert'. "Jim is one of our best agents. Is there a problem, sir?"

"Oh, no, no problem. I was only making sure before I let him inside. Thank you for your time." Billy hung up his desk phone.

Well, I guess that takes care of that. Can't arrest an insurance salesman, even if I'd like to.

Billy left the office. He had to go home, feed the dogs, give them fresh water, and get ready to head over to Junior's Farm.

LEO LESKO HUNG UP HIS phone, and debated with himself whether he should call Mickey Giambini, or, at least, Rizzo, and tell them about that phone call.

The caller ID on the Avalon Insurance phone read, "*Sardis County Sheriff's Office*".

The name that was given was the code name used by Moses Turley.

Making up his mind, he called Rizzo.

"Nothin' to worry about, Leo," said Rizzo. "Moses is on his way to New Orleans, following this Blake guy. That's just a Podunk sheriff checkin' up on him."

"Okay, Rizzo. Just filling you in."

"Glad you did, Leo. Good work. But forget about it. Not a problem."

The two men hung up.

THE FRONT DOORBELL was ringing. Katie and Phoebe, both dressed in the outfits that they bought that afternoon, came downstairs, and Katie opened the door.

Margo Sardis was on the porch.

"Aunt Margo! Come in!" said Katie.

"B'lieve I will, child, b'lieve I will," replied Margo, as she slowly crossed the threshold. "You surely look pretty, Katie!"

"Why, thank you, Aunt Margo! And you look very nice, too!"

Margo was dressed in a bright yellow blouse, with a dark blue, ankle-length skirt. Tennis shoes with velcro fasteners instead of laces covered her feet, but that was an accepted part of her age. Her gray hair was put up into a bun.

Phoebe was smiling shyly when Katie realized that she had not introduced the two.

"I'm sorry, Aunt Margo," said Katie. "I forgot to introduce..."

"...Phoebe Smalls," interrupted Margo. She held out her hand to Phoebe. "She's one of the cashiers at Mackie's, isn't she?"

"That's right, Miz Sardis," said Phoebe. "You sure do look nice tonight!" She took Margo's hand, and felt something surge through her. Her eyes widened, and she looked directly at Margo. "Yes, ma'am, I sure do. I always have."

"It's the same with him, child. He will come around, don't you worry," said Margo. "You need to know that you're bein' looked after, Phoebe. You're gonna be fine."

"Um...did I miss something?" asked Katie.

Phoebe looked confused. "You didn't hear Miz Sardis ask me if I still love Billy?"

Katie slowly shook her head as she replied, "Nooo...I only heard you answer, Phoebe."

"Oh," said Phoebe in a small voice. She put her hand to her mouth.

"Oh, now, you two stop it! It's not a big deal! And you'll see more tonight, so hush!" fussed Margo. "Now, where's the kitchen? Let's start cookin'!"

"CAROL GRACE, WILL YOU and Mary bring the charcoal and the starter fluid?" asked Alan. "I'll bring the grill."

The girls did what Alan asked as he lifted the barrel-shaped grill to the side yard just outside the kitchen windows.

"Mary, if you'll walk over to the garage, you'll see a coffee can sitting just outside the garage doors. It has water in it, with mesquite chips soaking. Will you bring it here?"

"Sure, Alan!" She ran to get the can.

"Carol Grace, I forgot the lighter. Will you go ask your mom for it?"

"Be right back!" she said, running toward the back door.

When the girls got back, Alan poured the charcoal into the grill, and showed the girls how to stack it for proper draw, then soaked the pile down with starter fluid. He took the long lighter and started the fire.

"Okay, one more thing from you two, and then you can do what you want," said Alan.

"Sure! What do you want us to do?" asked Carol Grace.

"Will you go get those plastic Adirondack chairs and bring all four around here? And bring a few more lawn chairs, too. Counting you two, we'll have seven people."

The girls brought the chairs as asked, helped Alan set them up, and then promptly plopped down into two of them. Little Bit sat between them, panting and looking happy.

Raising his eyebrows, Alan asked, "You two don't have anything else to do?"

Carol Grace wrinkled her brow at Alan. "We wouldn't miss this for anything!"

Smiling and shaking his head, Alan had no sooner sat down in one of the chairs, than Billy's personal truck rolled down the driveway. Little Bit barked once, then, recognizing the truck, sat back down.

Billy parked the truck in the turnaround, and climbed out. He had two six-packs of Guiness beer, and two twelve-packs of soda. "Hey!" called Billy. "Can I get a little help here?"

"Come on, girls!" said Alan. They walked over to Billy's truck.

"Hi, Sheriff," said Carol Grace.

"Hello, Carol Grace," said Billy. He turned and saw Mary. "And hello to you, ma'am. Do I know you?"

Mary smiled, and shook her head. "No, sir, we've never met. I'm Mary."

"Well, nice to meet you, Mary. Here, each of you can have a twelve-pack and a six-pack."

"Take them in the house, girls, and stick them in the refrigerator, please," said Alan.

Little Bit ran up to Billy, and started jumping. "Well, hello to you, too, pup-pup!" Billy ran his hand over the puppy's head and patted her side. "It's good to see you, too."

The men began walking over to the grill.

"Carol Grace named her 'Little Bit,'" said Alan. The men sat down.

The screen door on the back slammed, and the two teens came over and sat in their chairs while the men chit-chatted.

Soon, Billy looked at Mary. "Are you sure we've never met, Mary?"

Smiling, Mary nodded. "Positive, Sheriff."

"Do I know your parents?" asked the sheriff.

Alan and Carol Grace shared a look and a smile.

"I think you know my mom," said Mary, still smiling.

"Really? What's her name?" asked Billy.

Mary said, "Well, Sheriff, there she is. She'll be glad to tell you."

Billy turned. Phoebe was coming down the back steps. She was dressed in white shorts with a conservative length – three inches above the knee – and a neat, tucked-in dark blue T-shirt. Her hair was nicely cut and styled, and her makeup wasn't noticeable. She wore simple, open-toed sandals, and was smiling a shy smile. Katie came down the stairs behind her. She looked at Alan and winked.

Billy's mouth was open, and his eyes were wide. He had always thought that Phoebe was beautiful, but the simple outfit made her seem to be the perfect woman.

Carol Grace and Mary had wide smiles that threatened to burst into giggles any time.

"Hi, Billy," said Phoebe.

"F...fee...Phoebe?" stammered Billy.

Phoebe looked at Alan. "May a lady sit down, sir?"

Billy moved quickly, and gestured to the chair he had been occupying. "Please, Phoebe, sit here."

Phoebe moved to sit in the chair, and Billy held it steady for her. Once Phoebe sat down, Billy moved another chair closer to her, and sat in it, still staring wide-eyed at Phoebe.

Alan looked toward the kitchen. "Where's Aunt Margo?"

"She said she'd be out in a minute," replied Katie. "I think she was heading for the restroom. Everything's ready inside. We're having French fries, coleslaw, and baked beans. For the burgers, we sliced tomatoes and tore some romaine lettuce leaves. There are also onions for those people that don't want to be kissed good night."

"Wow, that's harsh!" said Alan. "Don't you think so, Billy?"

Billy was still staring at Phoebe, who was smiling. After a few seconds, Billy said, "Huh?"

"I said that your truck is on fire," said Alan.

"Oh, that's great, Alan," replied Billy.

Everyone else laughed.

"Katie, are the burgers in the fridge?" asked Alan.

Katie nodded.

"Looks like the fire's ready. Bill, you want to come help me with the meat?" said Alan.

"Sure." Billy stood, and looked down at Phoebe. "Will you excuse me?"

Phoebe nodded.

The men headed for the kitchen, while the ladies all huddled together.

Inside, Alan said, "Wow. Phoebe sure looks nice, doesn't she?"

Billy nodded. "Yes, she does. Why didn't you tell me that she would be here?"

"It was Katie's idea, Billy, but would you have come if you had known?"

"Probably not."

"There's your answer, then." Alan took out a platter of hamburger patties, and another platter of hot dogs. He handed the hot dogs to Billy. "You know, I think Phoebe still likes you."

"Phoebe still loves him. She never stopped."

Both men whirled around. Margo had just come into the kitchen.

"And I'll tell you something else, William Napier: Phoebe Smalls would just about move heaven and earth for you and you're too blind to see it!" Margo began making her way to the back door. "Just like a man to be too damn prideful to forgive. If you knew what was good for you, you'd make the wedding a double ceremony!" As she finished that last comment, Margo slammed the door behind her.

Both men stood speechless, staring after Margo's decisive exit.

"Okay...," said Billy.

Alan smirked. "I believe the lady has spoken, Bill."

"Well, Phoebe's going to have to change...," started Billy.

Alan held up his hand. "Stop. Phoebe was raped. Twice. She was unlucky enough to get pregnant both times, but chose to keep those children. Then, before she got sober, she lived with a guy that treated her badly, kept her drunk and drugged up, and gave her two more children. She's actually lucky that he died. She went through rehab, is clean and sober, and has shown the world the strength she has inside her. She's always welcome in our house. Keeping all that in mind, what, exactly, would you have her change, Billy?"

Billy was silent.

Alan slapped his friend on the shoulder. "She still loves you, man. She always has. She deserves a man that can share that strength and that love, a man to help her keep her strength and return that love, and that's all I'm saying on the subject. If you let her go this time, you have no one to blame but yourself. Now, c'mon, let's go cook some food!"

Billy followed his friend outside, deep in thought.

Billy searched his feelings. He often wondered why he had never married.

He realized that Alan was right.

He still loved Phoebe, and had for all these years.

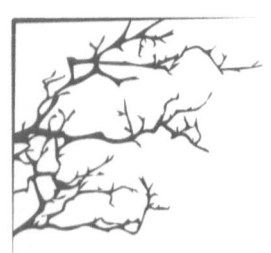

Chapter 14

When dinner was over, Katie suggested that they all move to the living room.

As everyone rose from the table, Margo said, "Carol Grace, why don't you and Mary go outside and play until it gets dark? That way, you won't have to put up with us stuffy old adults for too long. Maybe you can catch a few fireflies."

"Can we, Mom?" asked Carol Grace.

"As long as it's okay with Phoebe, it's okay with me. I even have a jar for you, if you'll let them go before you come inside," replied Katie.

"It's fine with me," said Phoebe.

Katie got the jar for the girls, and out the back door they went.

FLORE PARKED THE CAR well before they arrived at the house. A small dirt track let into the field they had to cross, and wasn't visible from the house.

"Okay, boys, let's cross this field, and hit that tractor shed," said Turley.

The four men got out of the car and slowly made their way across the field, hugging the woods as closely as they dared.

Moses Turley didn't want another rattlesnake encounter.

Finally, they arrived safely at the shed.

"Okay, keep quiet in the tunnel, and in the basement. We'll get our guns out of their hiding place, and go up through the basement door. Not a sound, understand?" Turley glared at Tolani when he said the last sentence.

"Don't worry, Mose, this ain't our first merry-go-round ride," said Tolani. "We'll take out whoever's in the house, and walk out the front door. Just like we owned the place."

Turley nodded, and opened the hatch that was behind the tractor. One by one, the men went down the ladder, and into the tunnel that led to the house.

"MAY I SAY SOMETHING?" said Billy, once everyone was in the living room.

Margo had sat in the comfortable rocker-recliner. Katie and Alan sat close together on the couch, and Phoebe had sat on one side of the love seat. Billy had a choice of two soft armchairs, a hard wooden rocker, or the other side of the love seat.

He had brought a soft drink for Phoebe, and, as he handed it to her, he accidentally touched her hand. That simple touch had triggered deeply hidden emotions inside him, and he felt like he had to do something about it.

"Of course you can, Bill," said Katie.

Billy looked down at the floor, then looked up at Phoebe. He was nervous, and it showed, but he was also determined, and that showed as well.

"The first thing I'd like to say is that I'm a fool," said Billy. "And I've been a fool since the day after graduation." He looked down at his twisting hands, then looked into Phoebe's eyes. "If I'd had any sense of being a man that day, I would have stood by your side, and supported your decision, Phoebe. Instead, I let foolish pride take over. It made me ignore what I felt for you, and I also let anger at the guy who raped you aim itself at you. I can't possibly make up for those years that I let my pride and my anger keep me from standing by your side. But I'd sure like to try." He knelt beside her, and took her hand in his. "Phoebe, if you'll have me, I'd like to spend the rest of my sorry life trying. I'll be a good husband, and as good a father as I can be to those children." He kissed the back of her hand. "Please say you'll let me try."

Phoebe, with tears in her eyes, opened her mouth to answer him, when she was interrupted.

"Ain't that sweet, Mose? He ast her to marry him."

Everyone turned to see Moses Turley and his men fanned out, holding handguns aimed directly at them.

"Yeah, too bad he won't ever hear the answer," said Turley. He turned his head to Alan. "And your time is up, Blake." Turley took aim, and pulled the trigger.

THE GIRLS WERE MOVING toward the woods. They could see that many more fireflies were hovering over the back part of the yard beside the woods, so they walked in that direction.

As they neared the huge old maple tree close to the tractor shed, Carol Grace caught movement in the corner of her eye. Whirling her head around and seeing the men, she grabbed Mary's wrist to stop her. Carol Grace put her finger to her lips in a "shhh" gesture, and pulled Mary around the maple tree.

"What is it, Carol Grace?" whispered Mary.

"There are some men out in the field, coming this way," Carol Grace whispered back.

The girls peeked around the tree, and saw the men go behind the tractor. They disappeared.

"They went down into the tunnel!" said Carol Grace indignantly. "How did they know about the tunnel?"

"What tunnel, Carol Grace?" asked Mary.

Carol Grace explained about the tunnel quickly. "Come on, Mary, we have to follow them!"

"Okay!"

The girls ran to the shed. Carol Grace found the handhold, and quietly lifted the hatch.

"Wow," whispered Mary.

Carol Grace put her finger to her lips again, then started down the ladder. Mary followed, and closed the hatch behind her.

The tunnel lights were on, giving a dim illumination. The girls crept along the tunnel quietly. When they came to the door to the basement, Carol Grace said, "They must be after Alan. We have to help."

Mary nodded. "You got it, Carol Grace."

The girls looked into each other's eyes, then Carol Grace nodded. She reached up and pressed the button that opened the door.

It slid open to an empty basement.

They crept up the steps, and slowly, quietly opened the basement door.

They were behind the men, and could hear every word that was being said.

The girls were now holding hands, and a faint blue glow was gathering around them.

Turley said, "And your time is up, Blake." The girls saw Turley take aim and pull the trigger.

The gun fired.

Simultaneously, both girls screamed, *"NOOOOO!"*

ALAN BLAKE PEEKED THROUGH squinted eyes, then opened them wide.

A small piece of metal with a rounded end was hanging in midair about a half inch from the bridge of his nose. Blue, smoky light was wrapped around the bullet, and looked to him like a fist was holding the bullet.

He looked past Turley and saw the girls. Everyone was looking at the girls now.

Carol Grace stood stiffly upright, with her right arm held straight up, palm facing out. Her left hand held tightly to Mary's right hand. Mary was a mirror image of Carol Grace – Mary was standing identically as Carol Grace stood, with her left arm held up, palm out. The girls were surrounded by a pulsing, smoky, blue bubble. Their faces held blank, almost dreamy looks.

Looking around, Alan saw that Katie, Phoebe, Billy, and even Margo had surprised looks on their faces.

Apparently, even the witches weren't expecting this.

The bullet in front of his face turned slowly around as both girls twirled their index fingers. When it was pointed back in Turley's general direction, the teens pulled their hands toward themselves quickly, and the bullet followed suit. It struck Turley in the right side. Turley grunted with the effort.

To his credit, Tolani was the first of the Turley crowd to come to his senses. When he heard Turley's grunt, he raised his own handgun and aimed toward the girls. Blasi and Flore say this, and raised their weapons as well. The three of them pulled their triggers. The kept pulling them until they had emptied their guns.

The girls still stood safely. Every bullet had been stopped in midair by the blue bubble, and now fell to the floor with a rattle.

Blue streamers came from the bubble, and wrapped each man in a tight grip. The four men then were lifted from the floor.

The girls, whose hands were still drawn inward from pulling the bullet into Turley, suddenly pushed their free hands out again. Each man was thrown hard through the living room windows, each to land awkwardly outside on the lawn.

Billy, Phoebe, Katie, and Alan all ducked their heads to avoid any flying glass, but there was nothing to worry about. The blue fingers that had held the bullet in front of Alan's face spread out into a thin shield that hovered over the grownups.

They turned to the girls. Still in their dreamlike state, they turned their hands around, and, still mirroring each other, wiggled their fingers in a summoning gesture.

Oh, dear God! thought Alan. *What are they calling?*

OUTSIDE, ON THE WEST side of the house, Flore and Blasi heard a loud snorting noise, followed by the weirdest howl they had ever heard in their lives. It raised goosebumps on them, and Blasi involuntarily pissed himself.

In the newly settled darkness, under the half-moon's light, something with green glowing eyes crept along the field, coming toward them.

The men couldn't move.

The creature approaching them had a long, almost serpentine neck. Its eyes faced forward, and its snout was almost lupine, with wolf ears and a mouthful of needle-like teeth. With so many teeth, the creature's mouth wouldn't close all the way, and it drooled constantly, but the drool never hit the ground – it disappeared before it fell that far. It had a long, thin lion's tail, and growing from its back were two large bat wings that it could fold against its body. Its skin appeared to be rough and pebbly, much like a rhinoceros's skin. When the creature uttered its snarl, its tongue came out, and appeared to be long and snakelike. It was big, approximately the size of a large tiger, but much bulkier.

When it was within a few feet of the men, the creature bunched its haunches, and sprang at the men.

It savagely tore Gino Blasi and Joe Flore apart.

TOLANI HAD BEEN KNOCKED lightly unconscious. He gradually became aware of what sounded like animals chittering. When he opened his eyes, he tried to scream, but no sound would come out.

Two creatures, one on either side of him, were squatting. They had long, spindly legs, and their knees were almost to their foreheads as they squatted. Their arms were just as long and thin, and were attached to barrel-shaped bodies. Huge bat wings grew from their shoulders. They had long, pinched noses with elongated nostrils, and bright, glowing, red eyes. The smiled constantly, and their smiles revealed rows of long, pointed teeth. Their movements were very birdlike.

Tolani thought he was dreaming all the way up until one bit him on the hip, and the other bit into his neck and severed his jugular. He found his voice again quickly, and, just as quickly, was silenced as he was eaten.

MOSES TURLEY HAD BEEN thrown the farthest when he had been thrown from the house. He landed halfway down the driveway, into the stand of trees that lined one side of it. He had missed hitting one of the trees, for which he was grateful, but the pain in his side from the bullet's slow entry hurt like a sonuvabitch.

Turley slowly sat up, then stood up. He heard Tolani scream, and he heard that scream abruptly cut off. He decided that he had a fast boat to catch for

South America, so he began stumbling toward the road, with the intention of getting into his car and driving away.

When Turley reached the road, he looked across at the trees that he and his men had hidden in when they first scouted the property. Something was off about them, but he couldn't put his finger on what it was.

Turley moved closer to the trees, looking them over to try to figure out what was different about them.

Then he saw it.

A couple of green glowing things were about twelve feet above him. He peered closely at them in the darkness.

A lighter shadow separated itself from the trees and stepped forward. In the dim half-moon light, the shadow coalesced into a being. It was approximately fifteen feet tall, not twelve, and had horns. Its arms were as big around as a man's body, and sharp, pointed claws extended from the ends of its fingers. Its ears were pointed, it had a beard. When it smiled, its teeth were many, and appeared needle sharp. Its eyes glowed with green fire.

Turley stood frozen as the creature reached for him. When it began squeezing him, Turley began screaming. He screamed until the huge creature bit off his head, and silenced Turley forever.

IN THE FIELD, THE GROUND under Turley's car became intangible, and green mist began lifting from underneath. The car slowly sank into the mystic hole underneath it, and the ground closed back over the top of the car, which was never seen again.

INSIDE THE HOUSE, THE girls were still wrapped in their protective bubble. With dreamy voices, they said in unison, "It is done. The citizens of Hell have eliminated the enemies. The Sardises will now perform the spell of protection, and we will restore the home."

Margo and Katie stood to do what was requested, and in a few minutes, the blue balls of power had spread from them, and settled over Junior's Farm.

The girls closed their hands into fists, and pulled the fists to their chests. Each window that had been broken by Turley's men were pulled back into their frames, and reassembled as if they had never been broken.

Then, the blue bubble vanished. Mary Smalls and Carol Grace Montgomery collapsed onto the floor.

They were sound asleep.

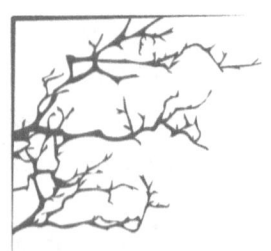

Chapter 15

Sunday morning, the two teens woke up with full memories of what had happened the night before. They sprang out of Carol Grace's bed, quickly brushed their teeth, and went downstairs to the kitchen.

Margo Sardis was cooking some breakfast and waiting for them.

"Hi, Aunt Margo," said Carol Grace.

"Mornin', girls," replied Margo. "Would one of you please hand me that basket? The biscuits are ready."

Carol Grace handed the old witch the basket, and sat down at the table. Mary joined her.

"Aunt Margo, where's Mom? And Phoebe?" asked Carol Grace.

"They've all gone to town. The sheriff is rousting out somebody from the county clerk's office to come to the courthouse and issue a couple of marriage licenses. Then, the sheriff is going to either find a willing judge, or arrest a preacher long enough to come out here and perform two marriages."

"*Two* marriages?" asked Mary.

"Yep. Seems like the sheriff finally figured out that he loves your mama more than he loves his pride."

The kitchen was quiet as Margo finished cooking breakfast.

"I reckon we'll help ourselves. When your parents get home, they can he'p themselves, too," said Margo. "So I guess we'll have to leave a little bit for them, won't we, girls?"

Both girls nodded. Each took a bite of egg with their right hands, then a bite of bacon with their left. They were mirroring each other again, and they didn't even notice.

Margo noticed.

"So, girls," said Margo conversationally. "What was that last night?"

"We don't know," said Mary.

"We just noticed this week that we could do things," added Carol Grace.

"But, it seems stronger when we're together," said Mary.

"Let me tell you a little something, Carol Grace," said Margo, and told them about the Sardis family's witching power. "But, I've never known one of us to be able to control creatures of Hell." She turned to Mary. "Which makes me wonder something, Mary. Who, exactly, *is* your father, child? And why do your powers grow stronger when you're together? You're a matched pair, somehow, and you mirror each other. But, instead of reflecting, you enhance." She shook her head. "I'm really gonna have to do some diggin' on this one. And I have to teach you two how to control this power better."

The sound of car doors slamming could be heard from outside.

Margo rose and walked to the window. "Looks like Sheriff Billy found what he needed. They brought Judge Lucas with them."

She turned to the girls, and motioned them toward the door. "Well, come on! We got weddings to tend to! We'll worry about wild powers another time, girls!"

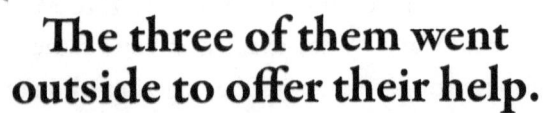

The three of them went outside to offer their help.

You're ready for book 3 in the *Tales Of Sardis County* series: *The Devil's In The Details – A Tale Of Sardis County*. It's available at your favorite eBook seller.

About The Author: T. M. Bilderback is a former radio announcer with a number of story ideas running around inside his head, most based on, or inspired by, classic songs. The author currently resides in Tennessee, and is writing feverishly in order to banish these stories from his head and into book form, before they drive him screaming into the street.

Other works by T. M. Bilderback

<u>Nicholas Turner</u>

If You Could Read My Mind

<u>Justice Security</u>

Mama Told Me Not To Come

Someone Saved My Life Tonight

Jackie Blue

Wake Me Up Before You Go-Go

Saturday In The Park

MacArthur Park

The Little Drummer Boy

The Night Chicago Died

Jim Dandy

Cow Patty

Hell's Bells

<u>Tales Of Sardis County</u>

Don't Come Around Here No More

Junior's Farm

The Devil's In The Details

I'm Your Boogie Man

<u>Colonel Abernathy's Tales</u>

The Lion Sleeps Tonight

Heart Of Glass

<u>Other Stories</u>

The Wreck Of The Edmund Fitzgerald

Gold

Hot Child In The City

Eli's Coming

<u>Other Novels</u>

Empty Eyes

<u>Story Collections</u>

Greatest Hits

Don't miss out!

Visit the website below and you can sign up to receive emails whenever T. M. Bilderback publishes a new book. There's no charge and no obligation.

https://books2read.com/r/B-A-KAW-GNIY

BOOKS 2 READ

Connecting independent readers to independent writers.